ONCE UPON

A *Curse*

E. D. BAKER

SCHOLASTIC INC.

New York Toronto London Auckland Sydney
Mexico City New Delhi Hong Kong Buenos Aires

ISBN 0-439-80684-4

12 11 10 9 8 7 6 5 4 3 2   5 6 7 8 9 10/0

Printed in the U.S.A.   40

First Scholastic printing, October 2005

The text was set in twelve-point Garamond.

This book is dedicated to Ellie for being my first reader and critic, to Kimmy for being so supportive and to Nate and Emiko for their enthusiasm. I would also like to thank Victoria Wells Arms for her questions and insight.

One

When I was a little girl, I never gave much thought to doing magic. I'd watch my aunt Grassina perform it every day and she never seemed to have any problems. When I started practicing magic, I expected it to be as easy for me as it had been for her. I couldn't have been more wrong. My first attempts at magic were a series of small disasters. I made crab-apple tarts that grew claws and pinched us. My cleaning spells were so strong that my bed made itself even when I was in it, and a whirlwind swept up everything I dropped, including my shoes and hair ribbons, dumping them in the dung heap behind the stables. I became a frog because of one kind of magic, while another kind turned me back into a frog at the worst possible times. Sometimes my magic didn't do what I'd intended, sending me to the dungeon or making me prematurely old. When dragon steam enhanced my magic and I became a powerful witch, I thought that my problems with magic were over, but once again, I was wrong. Suddenly I had bigger problems to face—problems caused by magic that I soon learned only magic could fix.

◌ℐ

I'd been visiting my aunt Grassina's workshop in the dungeon every day for the last few weeks and I had almost finished studying her parchments and the books she'd brought down from the tower rooms. With only a few more left to check, I was getting increasingly frustrated since I hadn't found a single spell that would help me.

When I'd arrived in the dungeon that morning, Grassina had dashed out of her room without saying where she was headed. Knowing her, she probably had some sort of mischief planned. I would have followed her to see what she was up to if I hadn't had something more important to do.

Massaging my forehead with one hand, I pushed the parchment aside with the other. I was tired of sitting in the dungeon. It wasn't as bad as it could have been, since there were plenty of candles and I'd dressed warmly, but the candles kept sputtering and going out, and the stink of decay was so strong it made my head hurt.

Something ran over my shoe, and I jerked my foot under my chair. *It's probably Blister,* I thought, shuddering. Once, before she changed from being the kind and gentle Green Witch to being the nasty, bewitched self she'd been for the last year or so, Grassina had kept a small, inoffensive, apple-green snake that had never bothered anyone. Now she shared her room with an old gray rat she'd found in the dungeon—Blister. He smelled awful, his fur was patchy and his naked tail was covered with sores, but his worst feature was his disposition, which was as nasty as my aunt's. I didn't mind the chill of the dungeon, the magic fogs that drifted from room to room or even the ghosts who popped in unexpectedly. Blister was a different story, however, since he loved tripping me and jumping out of shadows to startle me.

For the hundredth time, I thought about creating my own witches' lights so I wouldn't have to strain to see the words on the pages and the creatures that lurked in the darkened corners of the room. I knew better, however, because this was my aunt's workshop and she didn't like anyone doing magic in it except her. She was always nasty, but she was even worse if you did something she didn't like, which is why I'd gone to the dungeon in the first place. The feeble light from her flickering candles would have to do.

I'd been looking for a cure for the family curse for over a year. My aunt had been its most recent victim, and if I didn't do something about it before my sixteenth birthday, I might fall prey to it as well. Like our magical abilities, the curse had been passed down from generation to generation. It had started when my long-ago ancestor Hazel, the first Green Witch, had given out everlasting bouquets at her sixteenth birthday party and hadn't brought enough for everyone. A disappointed fairy had cursed her, saying that if Hazel ever touched another flower, she'd lose her beauty as well as her sweet disposition. Unfortunately the spell hadn't ended with Hazel, who had died centuries before I was born. Women in my family learned to stay away from flowers, with life-altering consequences if they didn't. They not only became ugly to look at, they turned so nasty that hardly anyone could stand them.

I finished reading another parchment and sighed. One more collection of useless spells for turning sows' ears into silk purses and lead into gold. The last spell, so long and involved that it had almost put me to sleep, had explained how to make mountains out of molehills.

"Almost finished, Emma?" said a high-pitched voice. My friend, a bat named Li'l, peered at me from the ceiling where she hung upside down.

"It shouldn't be long now," I told her. Rolling the parchment into a tube, I set it beside the others that I'd already studied. I was reaching for the last two, when I heard scratching at the door. "Grassina's back," I said, pulling my hand away.

My magic had improved remarkably since the day I had learned that I had the talent. Not only had I become a Dragon Friend, but I'd also become the Green Witch after Grassina lost the title. I could do a lot of things that I would once have considered impossible. Now I knew who was standing on the other side of a door without opening it. This was particularly handy when I was trying to avoid talking to my mother.

The scratching came again.

"Why would Grassina scratch the door?" Li'l asked.

"Good question." I reached for the latch and had opened the heavy wooden door only a few inches when it smacked into me, and an enormous lizard bounded across the threshold. At least seven feet long, the stocky creature's body seemed to fill the room. It raised its head to hiss at Li'l, but didn't pay any attention to me.

Li'l shrieked and flew to the ceiling, trying to hide in the cracks between the stones. The lizard cackled and its edges grew fuzzy, then suddenly my aunt was standing in its place. "Why are you still here?" she asked me. "I thought you were almost finished."

"I would have finished days ago if you had more light."

"There's enough light in here to do *my* spells, but if it stops your whining, I'll give you your rotten witches' lights. Anything to get rid of you sooner." With a wave of her hand and a few muffled words, Grassina sent a flurry of small globes bouncing against the ceiling. Instead of the rosy glow her witches' lights had made before she changed, these cast a sickly shade of green, making us look mortally ill.

A fuzzy little animal with a stubby tail and tiny ears scurried across the table. The creature squeaked as it ran off the edge and fell to the floor, where it lay on its back, twitching. Although it was about the size of a mouse, it didn't look like any I'd ever seen. "What is that?" I asked my aunt.

"A hamster," she said. "I saw them on my travels once. It used to be a spider, but hamsters have more meat on them. Being a lizard makes you hungry."

"That's disgusting!" I exclaimed.

"Do you really think so?" Grassina asked, her eyes brightening.

I looked up when one of the witches' lights went out. An ugly brown fog smelling of rotting vegetables was smothering the lights one by one. Grassina darted across the room to a barrel and rolled it to the center of the floor. The fog had almost reached the last witches' light when she muttered a few words and the barrel began to shake. Hissing like an angry snake, the barrel swelled as it sucked the fog through a small opening in its side. When the last wisp had disappeared, Grassina rammed a plug into the hole and rubbed her hands together. "Good!" she said. "I could use more of that."

"What do you need it for?"

"This," she said, stomping to her workbench and

uncovering a bowl filled with lavender dust. "I distill the fog and collect the residue."

"What does it do?" I asked.

"None of your business," she said, slamming the cover back on the bowl. "You're too nosy for your own good. I think you'd better leave. I'm sick of seeing your face around here."

"I'm not finished yet. I have two more parchments—"

"Here, take them," she said, snatching the parchments off the table and tossing them to the floor. "And don't come back!"

Li'l fluttered from her hiding place in the ceiling while I picked up the parchments. We'd hardly crossed the threshold before the door slammed shut behind us.

"At least you got the parchments," said Li'l, landing on my shoulder. "I thought she didn't want them to leave her workshop."

"That's what she said when I first asked to see them. It's the only reason I didn't take them upstairs before this. Unfortunately these probably won't be any more helpful than the others. I guess I'm going to have to look somewhere else."

"Where else can you look?"

"That's a good question," I said. "My sixteenth birthday is next week and I have to find a counter-curse before then. Father has scheduled his tournament to start the day before. He says it's to celebrate my birthday, but I think that's just an excuse. He's invited Eadric's parents and half of their kingdom, so I think he's hoping to impress my potential in-laws before any marriage contract is signed."

Li'l looked puzzled. "Why do you have to find the counter-curse before your birthday?"

"Because the curse could change me anytime after I turn sixteen. If that happens, there won't be a Green Witch to protect the safety of Greater Greensward. At least Grassina had me to take her place, but I don't know anyone who could take mine!"

"There you are!" my mother called as I closed the dungeon door behind me. "I can't imagine why you spend so much time in that horrid place, but then you always were peculiar."

Hearing my mother's voice, Li'l slipped off my shoulder and fluttered toward the darker recesses of the corridor. I couldn't blame her for being afraid of my mother.

"I was visiting Grassina's workroom," I said, hoping to distract my mother from the fleeing bat.

Mother looked as if she'd swallowed something bitter. Since the curse had taken effect, she'd avoided my aunt as much as she did my grandmother.

I nodded to my mother's lady-in-waiting who was hovering close enough to hear her name called, but far enough away to appear discreet.

"Your Highness," she replied, curtsying lower than she used to before I was the Green Witch. Being a princess hadn't meant nearly as much as being the most powerful witch in the kingdom, and I now received a lot more respect than I ever had before.

Cradling the parchments in my arms, I joined my mother as she entered the Great Hall. "I told you," I said, "I'm looking for a cure for the family curse. Grassina has been letting me look through her books and parchments."

"Have you found anything?"

"Not yet."

"I'm not surprised. If all the witches before you weren't able to come up with a cure, what makes you think you can? Don't get an inflated opinion of yourself, miss, just because you're the Green Witch."

"I won't, Mother." I certainly wouldn't with her around. "I just think that they might not have looked hard enough or in the right places."

"More likely there's nothing to find. You're wasting your time when you should be seeing to your new gowns. You'll be meeting Prince Eadric's parents next week when they come for the tournament and I want you looking your best, although there isn't much we can do with someone as tall and gangly as you. The seamstress will need all the time she can get to make you present-able, so I want you to go see her now."

"What I'm doing is very important—"

"Getting married is very important, and if you don't make a good impression on your future husband's parents, there may not be a wedding. We're going to have to use every trick we can to make them like you, and it's not going to be easy."

"I still haven't told Eadric I'd marry him."

"But you will soon, if you know what's good for you," Mother said, narrowing her eyes.

I left my mother with the promise that I would see the seamstress as soon as I could, but I had no intention of going straight there. Fittings were torture as far as I was concerned because my mother always showed up to point out my physical shortcomings as if I were the work of an inept sculptor.

I hadn't told anyone why I'd put off answering Eadric. Even he didn't know the real reason, although he'd made me promise to give him my answer at the tournament. I was afraid it wasn't going to be the answer he wanted to hear. Although I knew I loved him, I wasn't sure that I should get married. It was one thing to marry the man you love with the idea of living happily ever after, but it was something entirely different knowing that you could turn nasty any day and abandon your husband and children. I didn't want the same thing to happen to Eadric that had happened to my grandfather—left on his own when my grandmother Olivene had changed from normal to mean. My mother, who had so far avoided the curse by completely banning flowers from the castle, may not have thought it possible to find a way to end the family curse, but I had to believe that such a cure existed. If I was unable to end the curse, I had no intention of marrying anyone.

The tower rooms I now used had once been my aunt's, but I'd claimed them when Grassina moved to the dungeon. It was difficult to run up the uneven steps, and I had only reached the first arrow slit when Li'l dropped from the ceiling and landed on my shoulder. "What took you so long?" she asked. "I've been waiting here for ages."

"I was talking to my mother," I said.

"Your mother doesn't like me. She makes people hit me with brooms."

"She's afraid of bats. You'll just have to stay away from her."

"I'd be happy to, but she's hard to avoid. So are her eeks."

"What are *eeks*?"

"The people who try to bash me. They come running every time she covers her head and shrieks, 'Eek!'"

I smiled. "*Eek* isn't a title or a name. It's sort of like saying, 'Ick, a bug!'"

Li'l snorted. "That's insulting, isn't it? As if trying to bash me wasn't enough."

The moment we entered my chamber Li'l headed for the storage room where she usually slept, leaving me on my own. I hadn't made many changes to the tower after I had moved in, so it looked much the same as it had when my aunt lived there. A new workbench occupied the main room, replacing the one Grassina had taken with her to the dungeon. The two chairs and the table still sat before the fireplace; the dappled green rugs still covered the floor. Grassina had left her tapestries, the saltwater bowl and the living-crystalline bouquet behind, and I had seen no reason to move them.

I was comfortable in the tower and had all the space I needed to do my work as the Green Witch. Along with the title had come the ring on my finger and the responsibility of watching over Greater Greensward. Protecting our beautiful kingdom was a job I enjoyed. I used a farseeing ball to keep watch over the kingdom and toured the countryside by magic carpet every few weeks. Since becoming the Green Witch, I'd fended off an invasion from a neighboring kingdom, chased away a pack of werewolves, routed a trio of nasty trolls and taught a flock of harpies not to harass our villagers. I'd also taken on the responsibility of keeping the castle moat clean, which wasn't easy because Grassina insisted on dumping her trash into it. A witch's trash is different from that of an ordinary person, and sometimes noxious fumes and bizarre creatures emerged from the moat.

My aunt had been the kindest living adult I'd ever known, and I missed her real nature more than I could say, which was the other reason I had to find a cure for the family curse. Grassina was now as horrible as she had once been wonderful, and her nasty tricks were getting worse every day. She'd been terrible to Haywood, the man who had been her betrothed. He had lived with us for nearly five months after Grassina had changed, finally moving out when the tricks she played on him began to torment other people as well. He hadn't moved far, however, and still visited the castle now and then.

Grassina had driven away my mother's favorite ladies-in-waiting and more servants than we could afford to lose. Lately my aunt had even turned herself into strange beasts like the lizard I'd just run into, terrorizing the people and animals in and around the castle. Turning Grassina back into her old self would make everyone's life more pleasant.

I unrolled a parchment and settled down to read, but it proved to be as useless as the others. After glancing at the last parchment, I set them both aside and went to see Li'l. She blinked when I opened the door to the storage room. "Find anything?" she asked.

"Nothing useful, unless I want to remove rust or turn myself into a bird. I don't want to give up, but I don't know where to look next. I've talked to every bookseller at the magic marketplace, I've gone through my grandmother's books and parchments, and now I've looked at all of Grassina's—and I haven't found anything I can use."

"What about Vannabe's cottage? Mudine left a lot of good books there."

When I was fourteen, Li'l, Eadric and I had been imprisoned in a witch's cottage deep in the enchanted forest. A previous occupant had left her books of magic spells behind. The spells had been reliable, and I'd used a number of them before I learned how to create my own. Remembering that book, I felt a surge of hope. If the other books were just as helpful, perhaps one of them might contain the information I needed. "That's a good idea," I said. "If I go now, I can be back before dark."

"You sent the magic carpet to be mended, remember?" Li'l said. "How are you going to get there?"

I was about to answer when I glanced out the window. A dove was flying past the tower, the bronze-edged pattern on its wings distinctive in the bright summer sun. I leaned against the windowsill to watch the bird. *I wish I could do that,* I thought as the dove swooped and turned.

I loved trying new spells. Because Eadric had been involved in the original spell that had turned me into a frog, every time I had turned into one he had as well. However, once my power had become strong enough and I was better able to control it, I could turn into other creatures without changing Eadric. "I think I'll fly." I climbed onto the window ledge and recited the spell from the parchment.

> Fleet of wing and sharp of beak,
> Turn me to the shape I seek.
> When I say the final word,
> I will be a feathered bird.

My magic was stronger now, so the change was swift and painless. I no longer felt queasy when I changed from my human form to that of a creature, although the difference in perspective was still disorienting. I spread my wings and saw that I was covered with pale brown feathers. I had turned into a dove, the last kind of bird I'd seen. Cocking my head, I bent down to examine my orange feet tipped with small, sharp talons.

I'd watched birds before, of course, so I didn't think that flying could be too hard. After all, it didn't take baby birds long to learn, and I was certainly smarter than a sparrow. Raising my wings, I brought them down in a short, sharp movement. I was thrilled when my feet rose from the ledge, but raising my wings again forced me back down. *There must be some trick to this,* I thought.

Beating my wings once more, I moved out the window and found myself high above the moat. Surprised, I forgot to flap and dropped like a stone, remembering to flap again when I was only a few feet above the water. A long, gray tentacle shot through scum floating on the surface, its leaf-shaped tip brushing my tail. I beat my wings again, zigzagging up and down, trying to stay out of the monster's reach. Grassina must have dumped more trash into the moat, but I couldn't do anything about it until I got back.

I was over dry land again when I discovered that if I twisted my wings and folded them partway, I wouldn't force myself down each time I raised them and could finally fly like a real bird. I experimented, soaring higher than the castle tower and swooping low to skim the meadow grass. A sunny day with only a gentle breeze nodding the buttercups that edged the farmers' fields, it was the perfect day to practice flying.

Two

$\mathcal{D}$ark clouds were scudding across the sky by the time I saw the enchanted forest. Hoping to find shelter before the rain began, I fought an ever-strengthening breeze. The leaves on the trees were dancing, exposing their paler undersides, when I reached the forest's edge. Even on sunny days, the interwoven branches of the ancient trees prevented most of the sunlight from reaching the forest floor. The forest was even gloomier when the day was overcast.

I hadn't been in the forest long before I passed a green-skinned nymph slipping into a pond. A pair of unicorns huddled under a sheltering tree. I was still watching the unicorns when a griffin flew past, buffeting me with its eaglelike wings so that I had to fight to regain my balance.

Winging my way through the forest, I studied the trees, trying to find a familiar landmark that would lead me to the witch's cottage. I finally spotted a singed tree that I recognized and was able to get my bearings. It wasn't long before I reached the clearing and saw the cottage, looking much the way I remembered it, although the roof seemed to be in better repair.

Noticing the smoke escaping from the crooked chimney, I realized that someone was inside, and I had to force myself not to flee. I reminded myself why I was there. Although I knew I had to visit the cottage to examine the old books, the closer I got to it, the more nervous I became. While we were frogs, Eadric and I had mistakenly asked a witch named Vannabe for help, but instead of offering her assistance, she had kidnapped us, carrying us to this very cottage. Threatening to cut off our tongues and toes, she had locked us in a cage until I had found a spell in a book that opened every lock, latch and knot in the house. The thought that Vannabe might still live there almost made me turn around and go home, but I was no longer a helpless frog. As the Green Witch, I was more than a match for an aspiring witch like Vannabe.

When I heard voices coming from the cottage, I decided to investigate. I hurried closer to the house, skimming over the tops of the wildflowers that filled the clearing. The first drop of rain splatted on my wing as I landed on the windowsill.

Two women were seated inside, but neither one was the young, black-haired Vannabe. I couldn't see the face of the white-haired woman who sat at the table with her back to the window. The other one, however, was facing me, a tiny, thin woman with gray hair and a sour expression that matched the tone of her voice. "You promised me fresh air and sunshine," she said. "Ha! Fresh dust, fresh pollen, fresh manure—I bet you even have fresh mold in this dung heap, but no fresh air! Why would you live in such a hovel? My dog has a better home than this."

"It suits me. I invited you to visit because I thought you'd like the change. You're always complaining about the town."

"Who's complaining? I love the town. At least a witch can make a difference with her magic there. What can you do out here in the middle of nowhere?"

The white-haired woman sighed and turned around. I was surprised when I recognized her, although I shouldn't have been. After all, I had been the one to tell her about the cottage. Eadric and I had met her in the magic marketplace the year before while searching for magic beans. She had given us the beans in exchange for information about a jar of eyeballs that she claimed belonged to her. I'd seen the jar in the cottage when I was a prisoner, and I saw it again now, sitting on the table in front of her.

Unlike the day we'd met when she had one eye rattling loosely, she now had two eyes in her head, although they didn't match each other. The vivid blue eye seemed to fit

19

better; the brown eye with flecks of gold bulged from the socket. She had a large black mole on her cheek, and her toothless mouth seemed to collapse in on itself. Surprisingly her words were clear when she spoke. "I can *rest,* Dyspepsia. It was peaceful here until you came."

I needed to talk to these women and ask if they could help me. Jumping to the ground, I thought for a moment and recited my usual spell to become human. As I shot up to my normal height, everything seemed smaller and less intimidating. My skin felt stretched and pulled, prickling all over when my feathers disappeared. I sighed with relief.

Smoothing my hair with one hand, I knocked on the door with the other. A moment later it opened with a bang. It was darker inside, lit only by the fire in the fireplace and the pale light coming through the window. After a drizzling start, it was raining in earnest now.

"Would you look at that, Oculura," said the gray-haired witch from where she still sat by the window. "We finally have company."

"You were the bird on the windowsill, weren't you?" Oculura asked, motioning me into the room.

I nodded. "I didn't mean to eavesdrop …," I began, stepping into the cottage.

"Why not?" said Dyspepsia. "Listening in on conversations is often the only way to learn anything. I used to turn myself into a fly for that very reason."

"Until that man swatted you," said Oculura.

"He missed, which was a good thing for him. I would have been furious if his aim had been better."

"You would have been squashed if his aim had been better and in no shape to do anything about it."

"Hmph!" said Dyspepsia.

While the two women argued, I glanced around the room. It was neater than it had been before; the cobwebs and the old bird skeletons were gone, and the bat droppings had been scrubbed from the table and floor, which might have been why the room smelled so much better.

I looked toward the shelf where the books had rested. The dust was gone, and I was dismayed to see that the books were also missing. I was going to ask about them when Oculura turned to me, looking me up and down the way one might inspect a horse that was for sale. I half expected her to demand to see my teeth, but instead she said, "I know you from somewhere, don't I?"

I nodded. "We met at the magic marketplace. You gave us some magic beans."

"Hmm." Turning to her jar, the old woman selected two more eyes, popped out the ones in her head and stuck in the new ones. She blinked, then looked at me again. "That's better," she said. "I remember you now. You were with that nice young man. You told me about my jar of eyeballs."

I nodded again, unable to look away from her face. I

could swear that the black mole that had been on her cheek was crawling onto her chin.

"So," she said. "How were the beans? Did they do what you needed them to?"

"Yes," I said, dragging my eyes from her chin. "They worked quite well, thank you."

"And the young man? Is he still as handsome?" Oculura asked, looking through her eyelashes coyly.

I couldn't help it—my eyes flicked back to her chin. "He's the same as ever."

Oculura frowned. "Hasn't anyone ever told you that it's rude to stare?"

I could feel my face turning red. "I'm sorry, but your mole—"

"It's not a mole; it's a facial tick. I got it the first night I slept on that lousy bed," she said, pointing at the sagging mattress in the back of the room. The old witch tapped the tick with her finger, but made no move to dislodge the little black insect. "I like it now. It's grown on me—kind of like a beauty mark, don't you think?"

"Very nice," I said, trying not to grimace.

"Why are you here?" demanded Dyspepsia. "I know you didn't come just to get beauty tips from my sister."

"I'm trying to find a way to end a curse put on my family. I was hoping I could look at the books that used to be on that shelf."

"You can. I put them in the trunk with my own

books. You can look at those, too. Mind you, I wouldn't let just anyone look at them, but you told me about this place and I've been very happy here, despite my sister's complaints." Oculura looked pointedly at the gray-haired woman, then stomped to the trunk and flung open the lid.

"Take your time," said Dyspepsia. "It'll be nice having someone else around. All my sister does is play with those eyeballs of hers."

"Here you go," said Oculura, dumping a stack of books on the table. "You can look through these."

While the rain drummed on the roof of the cottage, I skimmed through the books, taking note of the more interesting spells. Dyspepsia sat in her chair by the window, complaining about her aching feet, the rain, the size of the cottage, her sister's lack of attention, the time of year and everything else she could think of. Ignoring us both, Oculura examined her collection of eyeballs, trying each eye one at a time, then in different combinations with the others.

"Each one sees things a bit differently," she explained when I glanced at her for a moment. Holding up a startlingly blue eye, she said, "This one belonged to a poet. Everything I see through it is very clear." She pointed at another floating in the jar. "A camp follower owned that one. It's always looking for a certain kind of man. And this," she said, reaching into the jar and plucking out an eye with a dark brown iris, "belonged to an old wizard who could see the magic in everything."

Oculura fished around in the jar and took out two milky-white eyes. I wondered how anyone could see with them. "These are my real seer's eyes," she said with obvious pride. Bending over the table, she popped out the eyes she was wearing and tucked the seer's eyes into the sockets. "Now give me your hand." Taking one of my hands in both of hers, she closed her eyes and hummed tunelessly, then said, "You're having a tournament at your castle, and you're going to invite me! I accept. And I'll bring my sister. We're going to have a marvelous time. There will be jousting and food and some ill-used magic and—"

"What's that about magic?"

"But before the tournament you're going on a long trip."

"I am?"

"Yes," she said. "Just don't ask me where. These eyes are old, and they tire easily."

"What was that you said about ill-used magic?" I asked as she changed her eyes again.

"You should have asked while I had those eyes in. It's too late now. I can wear them for only a short time before they need to rest. Would you like to see any others?" Oculura picked up the jar and swirled the liquid inside. The eyes swirled, too, and I thought they looked a little queasy. "I can show you my first eyes if you'd like. They were a beautiful, deep blue and matched my favorite gown. My ex-husband thought they were my best features. I have them here somewhere. My mother named me Oculura because of my beautiful eyes."

"You always were her favorite child," muttered Dyspepsia.

"She was a colicky baby," Oculura said, gesturing toward her sister. "So Mother named her Dyspepsia. She's had problems with her stomach her whole life."

"Problems with my stomach, problems with my feet, problems with men.... I never did get married," said Dyspepsia. "Never met the right man. What about you, girl? Anyone special in your life?"

"Yes, as a matter of fact." My chest tightened as I thought about Eadric. He'd gone back to Upper Montevista nearly six months before to help his father, and I missed him so much. He was due to come back the following week, but sometimes even a week can be an awfully long time.

"Was it that handsome young man?" asked Oculura.

I nodded. "That was my Eadric," I said, trying to look cheerful.

It didn't take me long to finish going through the books, simply because there wasn't much in them that interested me. I kept hoping up to the very last spell in the very last book that there might be something....

"Find anything that you can use?" Oculura asked, dropping an eyeball back into the jar.

I sighed. "Not a thing," I said as I set the last book aside. "Now I don't know what to do. I've looked every place I can think of, but there hasn't been anything."

"Hmm," said Oculura. "You did say it was a curse, didn't you?"

"That's right. It affects the girls in my family after they turn sixteen."

"And you're not sixteen yet?"

"I will be next week."

"Then if I were you, I'd talk to my sister."

"But I don't have a sister."

Dyspepsia snorted. "She doesn't mean your sister; she means me! I used to specialize in curses. I had to give them up, though. Curses take a lot out of you. You have to be really worked up to cast a good, strong one. All that anger made my stomach hurt more."

"So you know a lot about curses, including how to end them?"

"Of course I do, and I'd tell you, too, if only…."

"If only what?" I asked.

"My feet really hurt. What I could use right now is a good foot rub."

"Foot rub? But I…."

"My own sister won't touch my feet, but I'd feel so much better if someone rubbed the ache out of them.

I'm sure I'd feel like talking then."

"Fine," I said. "I've never rubbed anyone's feet before. I suppose you'll have to take off your shoes."

"Of course, but my back hurts, so if you don't mind…."

I sighed and reached for her foot. *The things I do for my family,* I thought as I slipped off the old woman's shoe.

Fortunately for me, Dyspepsia knew what she was talking about. I was soon so caught up in what she had to say that I forgot about the stickiness of her stubby toes and the way her feet smelled like rotten cucumbers. According to her, there were only two ways to end a curse. You could either persuade the person who had cast it to remove the curse, or you could do whatever the curse dictated. Unfortunately I couldn't do either since I didn't know who had cast it or exactly what it said. True, I knew a fairy had cast it; but that made it worse, according to Dyspepsia, since bargaining with fairies rarely worked. However, if I could find out which fairy was responsible for the curse, I *might* be able to get her to end it. Failing that, I'd have to try the solution imbedded in the curse, although fairies never made anything easy. I'd need the exact wording, and even that might not be enough.

"First things first, however," Dyspepsia said. "If you can't find any record of what really happened, you're going to have to go back to when the curse was cast."

"But it happened hundreds of years ago."

"You'll travel over time instead of distance. If you're strong enough, you'll be able to control the forces involved. If you're not, well, the curse won't matter to you anymore. The spell itself is simple. Just modify a basic search spell using an object from your destination as a focus. Since you want to go to a different time, your focus object must be from that time. When you want to come back, include when you want to return to in your spell. You won't need a focusing object since you're from this time."

I set her foot on the floor and picked up the other. "Oh, before I forget," she continued, "you'll need something to give your spell a little oomph. Everyone has a personal preference. I knew a wizard who could harness lightning to make his spells stronger."

"How did that work?"

"I can't say. No one ever saw him again, so it either worked or blasted him into dust."

"I don't think I'll try lightning," I said.

"Good idea. But whatever you choose needs to be portable so you can use it to come back."

"Anything else I should remember?"

"Of course. You're heading for a different location in time, but your location on the ground will remain the same. If the curse was cast long ago, most buildings and places will have changed since then. You're going to have to work your spell somewhere that has changed very little, or you might appear in the middle of a wall or at the bottom of a pond. Keep in mind that it should be out of the way. It wouldn't do to pop into the Great Hall or the queen's chamber. If you want to get the information you desire, you won't want anyone to know who you are or why you're there."

"It sounds complicated."

"It isn't really. I'm sure you'll do just fine. Oh, one other thing—make sure you don't change anything when you go back in time. Any change then could have a big effect later. Everyone always gives the same example: if you kill your ancestor, you'll never have been born."

"That doesn't make sense. If I killed someone, and then I didn't exist, how could I have killed him in the first place?"

"Don't ask me. I don't understand the details, I just use the spell and try to be careful. Now about my feet...."

Three

The rain had stopped by the time I was ready to go. After taking my leave of the two sisters, I turned into a bird again. Flitting beneath the dripping branches, I tried to remember everything Dyspepsia had said and wondered how I'd ever make it all happen. Perhaps talking to someone who knew our family history and was familiar with the castle might help me locate an object that I could use as a focus. My grandmother could probably help if she wanted to, although the chances of that were slim even if I did catch her on one of her friendlier days. She was the oldest living direct descendant of the first Green Witch and probably knew more about her than anyone, so I would just have to risk her bad temper. My next stop would be the Old Witches' Retirement Community.

With the entire width of the enchanted forest ahead of me, I had plenty of flying time to think. Even so, when I finally smelled the perfume of the rose-covered cottages, I still didn't have any idea what I was going to say. By the time I spotted the gingerbread walls of Grandmother's home, I'd decided to come right out and ask her.

My stomach grumbled as I landed on the edge of Grandmother's garden, my beak almost watering at the thought of all that delicious gingerbread. I hadn't eaten anything other than a bowl of porridge that morning and I was beginning to feel a little light-headed. Drawn by the sugary scent of the cottage, I was hopping toward it, opening my beak to recite the spell that would turn me back, when something struck me from behind. I sprawled beak-first on the rain-soaked ground, pinned down by a warm, heavy object. "I like a meal that delivers itself!" a voice murmured into my ear.

I recognized the voice. It was Herald, my grandmother's old orange tabby and one of the most disagreeable cats I'd ever met. Yanking my beak out of the dirt, I spluttered and shouted, "It's me, Emma, you lousy cat. You'd better let me up right now!"

Herald snarled. "Lousy cat, am I? Considering your position, princess, I don't think you should have said that."

I gasped and tried to think of a banishing spell, anything to get the cat off me. Herald picked me up with his teeth, pinning my wings to my sides. I struggled to get free but he clamped his jaws harder. The cat had taken only a few steps when suddenly something barreled into him, knocking him to the ground. Herald growled deep in his throat, a curious sound that made me vibrate in his mouth.

"Let her go!" said a gruff voice. Herald bit down instead, sending sharp pains through my wings. "Fine," said the voice. "If you're going to be that way—get him, Metoo!"

The cat twitched. When he opened his mouth to yowl, I fell onto the wet grass and staggered to my feet, reciting the spell that would change me back. The moment I opened my eyes as a human again, I turned to thank my rescuer. A small brown-and-white dog had the cat by the back of the neck. It was Olefat, the wizard my grandmother had turned into a dog to punish him for tricking her.

"Thanks," I said.

Olefat blinked up at me, then deliberately opened his jaws and let the cat go. Still yowling, Herald ran up a tree and onto a branch, where he stopped to scratch himself with a frenzied kicking of his hind leg. Obviously Metoo, Olefat's parrot that Grandmother had turned into a flea, had reached his target. "That's one!" the little dog shouted as he turned and trotted toward the back of the cottage.

My grandmother had told me that she'd tied the curse she had cast on Olefat to one Grassina had used to make him tell the truth. As long as one spell lasted, they both would be in force. According to Grassina's spell, "Three selfless acts you must perform, to aid a stranger who's forlorn." Apparently Olefat was trying to break the truth spell. I was giggling when I started toward my grandmother's front door.

"Who's there?" screeched Grandmother as she shoved her cotton-candy curtains aside and popped her head out the window.

"It's me. I've come to visit."

"No, you haven't. You've come to pick my brain. Grassina told me about your search. Still looking for a way to end the curse, are you?"

"I have some questions to ask you that might help. Do you mind if I come in?"

Grandmother cackled. "Of course I mind. If I'd wanted to see you, I would have gone to the castle. I don't like visitors. They always expect me to talk to them and give them something to eat. They either stay too long or leave before they should; they snoop around and ask nosy questions. There ought to be a law against unexpected visitors. But you're here now, so I guess I'm stuck with you. Come in if you have to."

My stomach was grumbling again when my grandmother met me at the door. She scowled and said, "See, I told you so! You'll be wanting food now!" Without waiting for an answer, she turned and stalked off to the kitchen. Jabbing a finger at the bench by the table, she ordered, "Sit down," then slammed a mug of cider in front of me. While I wiped the cider from my face, she broke off part of the windowsill and tossed it onto the table. It was magic gingerbread, which stays fresh for years. Its gingery, sweet taste made my whole mouth tingle.

"Now, what did you want to ask me?" Grandmother said as soon as I had a mouthful of gingerbread.

I hurried to swallow and nearly choked. Coughing, I took a sip of cider, then cleared my throat and said, "What can you tell me about Hazel, the first Green Witch?"

"Nothing!" Grandmother snapped. "There, I answered your question. Now go home and leave me alone."

"Surely you know something about her. Of course I could just go ask Grassina. She always says that she's forgotten more than you ever knew." The curse had made my aunt and my grandmother so much alike that they were always trying to outdo each other, a fact I'd learned to turn to my advantage.

"She did, did she? What a liar. Say, she hasn't gotten a lizard for a pet, has she? I found one hunting moles in my garden the other day. It took off before I could get a good spell going, but something about it made me think of your aunt. I had to come up with a new spell to replant my rosebushes. The ugly brute tore them all out of the ground."

I sighed. My grandmother did have beautiful roses, something that was of course forbidden at our castle. "Grassina doesn't have any new pets aside from a smelly rat," I said, "but she likes turning into a big lizard so she can terrorize everyone in the castle."

"She would, wouldn't she?" said my grandmother. "I thought it looked like Grassina. It smiled at me before it ran off."

"You were going to tell me about Hazel, the first Green Witch," I prompted.

"I was, was I?" Grandmother shrugged. "Might as well. Can't have you thinking that nasty daughter of mine is the only one who knows our family's history. Hazel's father was King Grunwald the third or maybe the fourth. He built the castle you live in now. They say the magic came down through her mother's side, but then it would have to, wouldn't it? The only ones in our family who have the talent are the girls."

"What part of the castle did King Grunwald build?" I said, remembering Dyspepsia's comment about finding the right location.

"The oldest part, of course. Use your head, girl! The whole back half was added on later by your great grandfather and so were many of the towers."

"Would any of his possessions still be in the castle? A suit of armor, perhaps, or a piece of furniture?"

"There might have been before your mother became

queen, but she had the castle cleaned from top to bottom the year after she married your father. The nitwit even had servants scrubbing out the dungeon. I doubt there's anything in there older than two hundred years. She always has preferred new things over old."

"I meant to ask you, are you coming to the tournament?"

"Of course I'm coming. You know I love tournaments. What tournament are we talking about?"

"My parents are putting one on next week. Eadric's parents are coming."

"Eadric who? Do you mean your pudgy friend with the big ears?"

"Eadric doesn't have big ears!"

"Ah-ha! So, it *is* him. I'll be there. Or at least I think I will. Let me get my scrying bowl so I can see and make sure."

I took another bite of gingerbread while Grandmother snatched an old, chipped bowl off the shelf. After pouring a dipperful of water into the bowl, she set it on the table. "Now don't yammer at me while I do this. I have to concentrate. Let's see," she said, leaning over the bowl so her long nose nearly touched the water. I couldn't see whatever she was looking at because her head blocked my view, but apparently she saw something. "Tournament … next week … will I be there? There's Eadric, big ears and all. There's your mother, looking prissy as usual. I see a couple of dotty, old witches. Wait, one of them's me. Yeah, I'll be there. And so will … say, look at this. There'll be some magical trouble at your tournament, girl. Something's going to go very wrong."

I nearly choked on the gingerbread again. When I could talk, I said, "Oculura mentioned something about that. What is it? Can you see?"

Grandmother sat back and glared at me. "I told you not to talk! How am I supposed to concentrate with you blathering away? Now let me look. I think it's—"

With a thump and a swish of his tail, Herald the cat landed on the table beside the bowl, then stuck his face in it and started lapping the water. Whatever picture Grandmother was studying disappeared in ripples.

"Darn cat!" Grandmother grabbed Herald and tossed him out the window. "Want a drink of water?" she asked me. When I shook my head no, she carried the bowl to the window and dumped it over the ledge. The water must have hit Herald, because he howled. My grandmother cackled. "Serves you right, you old sour-puss!" she said and slammed the bowl back on the table. "Say, I have some liver I've been meaning to cook for weeks. It has a nice, blue sheen to it now, so I'm going to boil it with a few turnips before it goes bad. I'm making beetle-wing biscuits, too. Care to stay for dinner?"

My stomach flip-flopped at the thought. "It's getting

late. I should go home before it gets dark," I said, scooting off the bench. "Thanks so much for your help."

Grandmother glared at me. "See, it's like I said. You're leaving just when I'm getting used to you being here. Well, good riddance, and don't come back soon!"

❧

I probably would have forgotten all about Grassina's newest moat monster if it hadn't tried to catch me again as I flew toward my tower window. Although its body was still hidden in the murky depths, its thick tentacles with their leaf-shaped tips were clearly visible, flailing in the air.

No normal creatures lived in the moat anymore because Grassina's previous monsters had eaten them all, so it wasn't surprising that this one was always hungry. Keeping an eye out for the tentacles, I recited the spell I'd used on the other monsters.

> Find the monster in this moat
> And send him far away
> To a place where monsters dwell,
> A place where he can stay.

I swerved out of the way when one of the tentacles whipped past me. Some spells take longer to work than others, and this one seemed to take an extra-long time. I was relieved when I heard a sucking, slurping sound and the thrashing tentacles disappeared.

My rooms were dark when I landed on the windowsill although torches burned in the streets of my favorite tapestry, which depicted a town and its marketplace. My golden canary trilled a greeting as I fluttered into the room, twittering in excitement when I turned back into a human.

"Lights," I said, flicking my fingers at the ceiling where witches' lights bobbed. Like most spells I used often, I no longer had to recite the complete spell out loud.

With the lights glowing gently overhead, I hurried to my bedchamber, intent on locating a special box. Although I had no idea where I could find a focus object from the past, I already knew just what I would use to strengthen my power. Hidden in a box in the bottom of my trunk was a small bottle containing dragon's breath, the most powerful substance I'd ever encountered. While dragon's breath was a key ingredient in a potion that had changed an otter back into a man, it had been dragon's steam—a heated form of their breath—that had enhanced my own magic, making me the most powerful witch in the kingdom.

Taking the box from the trunk, I lifted the silver lid. Pinks, blues, yellows and greens swirled in the gas that nearly filled the bottle. I slipped the little bottle into the pouch that I carried at my hip and reached for my warmest cloak. With the tournament less than a week away, I didn't dare waste time.

I locked the door behind me, keeping an eye out for any of Grassina's magic tricks, but I didn't notice the noise in the Great Hall until I'd reached the bottom of the stairs. It was a bit late for dinner, which meant that my parents probably had guests and were dawdling at the table. Unless I wanted to be drawn into their conversation and spend the rest of the evening with them, I'd have to slip past unnoticed.

I peeked into the Great Hall. The smell of roast pheasant would have tempted me once, but I could no longer eat meat, having been an animal myself. It was the reason I usually avoided eating with my parents now, since they didn't understand my reluctance and still tried to make me eat it.

Drawing my cloak around me, I hoped that keeping to the shadows would be enough, but the moment I stepped into the hall, my mother spotted me. "Emeralda," she called, using my full name. "It's so good of you to join us. Come see who's here."

I sighed and turned to face the raised table where my parents sat side by side, surveying the Hall. Seated on my father's other side was a middle-aged man with a pleasant face and sand-colored hair tinged with gray.

"Haywood!" I hurried to the table, hoping to avoid sitting beside my mother. Haywood had been a wizard-in-training before my grandmother had turned him into an otter, long before I was born. He'd been working on his magic ever since he had turned back into a man and was getting fairly good at it. "It's nice to see you," I told him. "Are you staying long?"

"Just a few days," Haywood replied. "I'm building a house by the river, and I still have a lot to do. I'll be back next week, though. Your father has invited me to his tournament."

"Wonderful!" I'd gotten to know Haywood during the months that he lived with us and had found him to be very likable. Even my mother's opinion of him had changed. He would have been welcome in our home anytime if it hadn't been for my aunt. "Have you seen Grassina?" I asked.

"Briefly," said Haywood. "She threatened to turn me into a hamster, which I thought was rather odd."

"She was probably hungry," I said. "You might want to fly home and avoid any lizards you see."

"Emeralda, come sit by me," my mother ordered, leaving me no choice unless I wanted to create a scene. I took my seat beside her reluctantly. It looked as though everyone was nearly finished, but my mother had the pages bring the platters around again. Fortunately having a guest meant that she might not notice when I chose only vegetables and a hunk of bread.

Mother's eyes narrowed when she turned to me.

"Where were you today? You know the seamstresses were going to fit you for your gowns."

"I was seeing to something important," I said.

"I hope this important matter doesn't prevent you from having your fittings tomorrow! You've wasted too much time already. Luckily for you, you missed your aunt's mischief making. Your father went hunting today. The hounds flushed a hare from the underbrush right away. Your father said that it led him a merry chase until the hounds finally ran it to ground. Then what do you suppose the hare did?"

"Got eaten by some half-wild dogs?"

Mother's eyes snapped. "It turned into a monstrous lizard that chased *them*. The horses were terrified and the dogs…. Well, see for yourself," she said, pointing to the corner of the room.

During meals, Father's hounds normally waited under the tables watching for dropped food or the occasional handout, so I was surprised to see them cowering in the corner with fearful eyes.

"Grassina did that?" I asked.

"And thought it was very funny when I confronted her. Your father is furious."

A squire who had come into the hall slipped behind the tables until he reached my father. They spoke for a moment, before Father turned to me. "It seems your prince Eadric has returned earlier than expected,

Emeralda. He's in the stable with his horse."

I hopped to my feet, nearly knocking a platter from a page's hands. "May I be excused?" I asked.

"Of course my dear," said Father.

Mother started tapping her fingers on the tabletop, a sure sign that she wasn't pleased. "He wasn't supposed to be back for another week. I hope his parents' plans haven't changed."

"I'll find out," I said and dashed from the room before she could think of a reason that I should stay. Once I was out of my parents' sight, I hiked up my long skirts higher than was probably modest and ran as fast as I could.

The animals had been fed, and the comfortable sound of horses munching their grain filled the stable. I peeked over the door of Bright Country's usual stall and saw Eadric brushing his horse until the stallion's white coat shone. Ferdy, Eadric's singing sword, hung from a nail on the wall, close to Eadric. Since the day when Eadric had been unprepared for the battle between Greater Greensward's army and the army of East Aridia, he'd always kept his sword nearby.

Eadric looked wonderful standing in the stall, his sleeves rolled up and his clothes muddy from a hard day of riding.

"Eadric," I said, and then the door was open and I was in his arms, which was exactly where I wanted to be.

Four

It was nearly an hour before I returned to my original errand. Eadric and I had spent a few wonderful minutes while Bright Country eyed us with disgust. When he finally snorted and said, "Get a stall," we stopped kissing and grinned at each other. Eadric looked different from when I'd seen him last, and I was surprised by how much he'd changed in a few months. He'd grown another inch or so and was now nearly as tall as me. His chin and upper lip were rough from stubble, and his curly, brown hair was longer than he used to wear it. What really surprised me, however, was that his paunch was almost gone and the muscles in his arms and across his chest had gotten bigger.

"How have you been?" Eadric asked, his voice a bit deeper than I remembered it.

"Miserable while you were gone. Wonderful now that you're back. And you?"

"So lonely that I couldn't stay away any longer. My

parents are coming next week. They wanted me to travel with them, but I told them I had to help a lady in distress."

"Oh, really? And who was the lady?"

"You. You did say you were miserable."

"Devastated."

"Good. I'd hate to think I lied to my parents."

"What else did you tell them?"

"That you're beautiful and exciting and the only woman with whom I could live happily ever after. That they'll like your parents, but your aunt Grassina is a little unusual."

"Aunt Grassina! I was on my way to see her when my mother stopped me. I have so much to tell you! I met Oculura's sister, Dyspepsia, who told me how we can learn about the curse, and now Grandmother is coming to the tournament where some magic is going to go wrong."

Eadric held up his hand and laughed. "Slow down! One thing at a time, please."

I started over again and told him about seeing Oculura, the witch we'd met at the magic marketplace, and her sister who used to be an expert on curses. He nodded and said, "How nice," but I could tell he wasn't very interested until I told him that I'd have to travel back in time to learn the actual words of the family curse.

"Really?" he said. "You can do that?"

"According to Dyspepsia I can. All I need is something that came from that time and something to make my power stronger. I already have the vial of dragon's breath, which has the strongest magic you can get."

Eadric rubbed his chin. "What time are we talking about?"

"The Dark Ages. That's why I need to see Grassina. Maybe she knows of something old."

"If you really think she'll help us, she must have changed since I was here last."

"She's gotten worse, if anything, but it's worth a try," I said.

"Wow," said Eadric, his eyes lit with excitement. "Going back in time! I never thought I'd do that."

"Eadric, you aren't going. It isn't safe. I have no idea what I'll find or even if it will work."

"Of course I'm going. You don't think I came back early to visit with your parents, do you? And I've heard what knights used to be like in the Dark Ages. One of them could kidnap you, drag you back to his castle and force you to marry him. You're not going without me."

"Are you threatening to drag me off to your castle?"

"If I have to," he said, trying out a wicked leer.

I knew there was no arguing with Eadric. I started to tell him about everything else that had happened to me since he left. I was still talking when we headed for the dungeon, and I had to cut short my description of Oculura's eyes as we reached my aunt's room. Grassina didn't answer when I knocked, although we could hear someone banging around. Curious, I opened the door a crack and peeked inside. A lizard once again, my aunt was chasing a hamster, her nails scraping the floor, her scaly tail slamming into the bench and knocking over the chair. The hamster squeaked and tried to run up the wall, falling flat on its back with a tiny thump. Grassina pounced on the helpless creature and snapped it up in an instant.

"Aunt Grassina!" I said, shoving the door open all the way. "Stop that right now! How can you eat those hamsters?"

"Oh, bother!" rasped Grassina in her lizardy voice. "Don't you have anything better to do than to spy on me? Hold on, I'm going to—*Brap!*" She burped, gave me a toothy grin and turned back into a human. "What are you doing here? How can I get any work done if you keep popping in?" She peered at Eadric in the dim light. "Who's that with you? It's not that dunderhead Eadric is it?"

"Hello, Grassina," said Eadric. "How have you been?"

"When?" she barked. "Be specific, boy."

"I wanted to ask you some questions," I began, "but if you're too busy—"

"Don't be silly. Of course I'm too busy. Go away and bother someone else."

"You sound like Grandmother. She didn't want to talk, either."

Sticking a grimy finger in her mouth, my aunt probed her teeth with her fingernail. "You went to see my mother? What about?"

"I had some questions about our family's history," I said. "Grandmother seemed to think she knew more about it than you did, but I thought I'd ask you, anyway."

"Huh," grunted my aunt. After examining her fingernail, she flicked something off it onto the floor. "Don't believe a word she says. That old bat can't remember her middle name, let alone family history. Besides, I know more than she ever did."

"Then you must know all about Hazel, the first Green Witch. Was her father King Grunwald the third or the fourth?"

"The third," she said, running her fingers through her hair until it stood out around her head like a squirrel's nest. "But his wife was a commoner. Don't stand there like an old stump—fetch me that bowl of powdered nightshade. You might as well make yourself useful while you're here." Going to her workbench, Grassina lifted the lid off a cold, iron cauldron and reached for a wooden spoon. "Now where was I? Oh, yes, Hazel. She liked plants. Had a real green thumb. What else did you want to know?"

"Would there be anything of Hazel's here in the castle? Or something that belonged to one of her parents?" I went to the shelf where my aunt stored most of her dried plants and took the containers down one at a time.

"Never seen anything like that. Why do you want to know?" Grassina glanced in my direction and pointed. "The nightshade is in the cracked bowl on the end."

"Just wondered." I took the bowl down and shook it. "You're almost out."

"Don't tell me that! I need five spoonfuls for the next step!"

"I don't think you have more than two here," I said, handing her the bowl. "What are you making?" Grassina caught me peeking into the cauldron and slammed the lid back on, but not before I'd seen that it was half filled with sparkly, lavender dust.

"None of your business! Now get out! I need more nightshade if I'm going to do this right, and I don't want you in here while I'm gone. You don't have any nightshade upstairs, do you?" she asked, squinting at me.

"No, sorry, I don't keep—"

Grassina snorted. "Well, you should. Never know when you're going to need it." Grabbing an empty sack, she hustled Eadric and me out of the room and waved her hand over her door to lock it. "And keep out!" she said, glaring at me before turning on her heel and steaming off down the corridor.

Grassina hadn't told me anything very useful, but I still wasn't ready to give up. Pointing my finger to light the torches on the wall, I gathered my skirts around me and sat down on the dungeon steps, leaving room so Eadric could sit beside me. "Maybe I could use a chip from one of the original stone walls as my focus," I said. "I could take it from one of the older sections and...."

A blue mist seeped through a door at the end of the hall, thickening until it took the form of an elderly man with long white hair and a regal posture. He drifted down the hall toward us, his refined features becoming more apparent as he approached. When he finally reached my side, he seemed to loom over me.

"Is something wrong, my dearest Emma?" asked the ghost.

I drew my cloak more tightly around my shoulders since the air was chilled by his presence. "Hello, Grandfather. I have a puzzle to solve, that's all. By the way, this is Eadric. I believe I told you about him. Eadric, this is my grandfather King Aldrid."

"I remember. I've seen him around the castle," said Grandfather, "although we've never officially met."

"Hello, sir," said Eadric. For someone who was talking to a ghost for the first time, he did very well. His voice was only slightly shaky and his cheeks only a little pale. My grandfather was charming even as a ghost—

he'd chosen to live in the dungeon when my grand-mother had fallen victim to the curse, and he had stayed on as a ghost even after he'd died.

"It's a pleasure to meet you, young man. Emma, you said you have a puzzle? How delightful. Perhaps I can help you."

"I hope so," I said. He already knew about my desire to find an end for the curse, so I told him what I'd learned from Dyspepsia. "I have something to make my power stronger, but I still need an object from Hazel's time. Grandmother said that my mother had all the old things thrown away. Hazel's father was King Grunwald the third. I don't suppose you know of an object from his reign that I could use?"

Grandfather rubbed his chin and frowned. "Grunwald the third, hmm. I don't know of anything from that time—"

I sighed. "Then I suppose I'll have to use a chip from a wall he had built."

"Oh my, no!" said Grandfather. "That might take you back years before the day you need to arrive. It should be from something that happened closer to that party, I suppose. I know someone who should be able to help you. Come back in the morning, and I'll try to have him here."

We left Grandfather with the promise that we'd meet him first thing in the morning. Eadric was yawning broadly when we left the dungeon, so we said good night, and he stumbled off to the bedroom he'd used before.

When I passed through the Great Hall, the room was empty except for the hounds still cowering in the corner, startling at every sound. Upstairs in my chamber, I crawled into my bed grateful for its comforting warmth, but I couldn't stop worrying about what I planned to do. Who was Grandfather bringing, and how could this person help me? What if the spell didn't work, and I didn't go anywhere or ended up in the wrong time? And even if the spell was successful and I reached Hazel's time, who knew what I would face?

Sleep was impossible as I thought about why I should go. If I couldn't find a way to end the curse and it changed me before I found someone to replace me as Green Witch, Greater Greensward would be without magical protection. Even if the curse never changed me, I'd have to spend the rest of my days trying to protect everyone I cared about from my crazy aunt and worrying that I still might be the curse's next victim. When I finally fell asleep, I dreamed of sharp-clawed monsters with teeth like daggers chewing up the trestle tables in the Great Hall where my entire family sat, waiting to be devoured.

I was up early the next morning collecting everything I thought might be useful on my trip: a piece of string, a candle stub, a vial of protective salve my dragon friend Ralf had given me and, the most important, the bottle of dragon's breath that I'd put in my hip pouch the day before. The string could always become rope; the candle, an ever-useful light; the salve, a great protector; and the dragon's breath, a way to get me there and back. I hung my smallest farseeing ball on a chain around my neck, dressed in a comfortable gown and warm cloak, fed my canary, then went to check on Li'l. My mother wouldn't need to know, as I figured on returning the same day.

"Where are you going?" asked the little bat from her favorite rafter.

"Into the dungeon for now. If everything works out, I'll be going to find the cure for the curse."

"Can I come with you?" she asked, fluttering to my shoulder.

"You can come as far as the dungeon, if you'd like, but after that I'll need to be on my own. I'm going to try to travel back in time, and I'm not sure what I'll find. I don't dare take anyone with me."

This time when I went to the dungeon, I took a witches' light tethered to me by magic. Lighting my way with a warm glow, it kept pace like a well-trained hawk, staying a few feet above my head. Eadric was waiting for me in the Great Hall, taking bites from a hefty chunk of cheese. He offered me some, but my nervous stomach gurgled and I decided not to take it.

Grandfather was already waiting for us in the dungeon with two ghosts I'd never seen before. Wary of strangers, Li'l hunched down on my shoulder, gripping my cloak with her claws. The room was so cold from the presence of three ghosts that I could see each puff of our breath. Even with the cloak wrapped around me, my teeth chattered and I had to listen hard to hear my grandfather.

After nodding to Eadric, Grandfather drew me to his side so that we faced the other ghosts together. "Emma, I'd like you to meet Sir Jarvis," Grandfather told me. The ghost wore a peaked cap, over-tunic and leggings that had long been out of fashion. His noble bearing would have been the same in any time period. "And this is his friend, Hubert. Hubert tells me that he worked in the stables of Grunwald the third." The ghost was stooped with age, his long hair straggled almost to his knees, his tunic was little more than a rag and his legs and feet were bare. The finely wrought chain that he wore around his neck seemed very much out of place.

"*King* Grunwald to you, youngster. You need to learn respect for your betters," said Hubert.

Sir Jarvis looked appalled. "Sorry, Your Majesty! Hubert hasn't been the same since guards came down a few months back and opened the trapdoor to the oubliette." The oubliette was little more than a hole in the cellar of the castle covered by a rusty, metal grate. It was where the old kings put prisoners who they wanted to forget. "Hubert was sure that they'd finally remembered him and had come to let him out. A bit late, if you ask me, but he has trouble with his memory even on the best of days. He forgets that only his bones are left in that pit, and the guards weren't interested in those. Hubert," he said, turning to his friend, "this is King Aldrid. You've met him before!"

"He's not the king!" grumbled the stooped ghost. "King Grunwald the third is the king and has been for as long as I can remember. I've worked in his stables since I was just a lad."

Sir Jarvis shook his head. "That was many years ago, Hubert! Limelyn is king now. This is his father-in-law, King Aldrid. He wants to ask you some questions."

"What kind of questions?"

"Actually," I said, "I'm the one who wants to talk to you, Hubert. I'm Princess Emeralda and I'm interested in King Grunwald the third. Can you tell me anything about him or his daughter Princess Hazel?"

"That I can. Princess Hazel is lovely, much prettier than you. She has the most beautiful golden hair, with eyes the color of robins' eggs and skin as smooth as cream. She has a green thumb and can grow anything she has a mind to. Why, I've seen her grow a potato vine up the stable wall that sprouted potatoes in less than a day.

Lots of talent our princess has; you can be sure of that! It was the little princess who gave me this medallion just before the big party," Hubert said, pulling the chain out from under his tunic. A silver disk spun on the end of the chain. "Said it was for bravery. I never took it off. Had to hide it or many's the time they would have taken it from me." Eyeing me as if I might try to grab his ghostly medallion, Hubert tucked it back under his filthy tunic.

"It was a lovely medallion," I said. "And it was very kind of the princess to give it to you. What about King Grunwald? What was he like?"

The aged ghost's shape wavered, his form growing faint, then more distinct. "Why are you asking all these questions? You aren't a spy, are you? The king doesn't take kindly to spies! I'll call the castle guards; that's what I'll do. They'll throw you in the oubliette, and you'll never get out!"

"That's all right, Hubert," said Sir Jarvis, patting the older ghost's arm. "Calm down now, old fellow. There are no spies here!" Hubert muttered to himself while his friend turned to Grandfather and me. "Hubert spent his last days in the oubliette. Grunwald the fourth had him tossed down there when something went missing. I think Hubert was caught someplace he shouldn't have been, but he certainly paid the price. The oubliette was a terrible place to die."

"I'm not going back there!" shouted Hubert. "You can't make me!"

I couldn't blame him.

"There, there, Hubert. No one is going to make you do anything. I think it's time for us to go. Good day, Your Majesties," said Sir Jarvis, bowing to Grandfather and me.

"What did they say?" Li'l piped up as the two ghosts faded into blue mist and floated down the hall. "I could understand him all right," she said, waving her wing at my grandfather, "just not those other two."

"Really? And can you understand Li'l?" I asked Grandfather.

He nodded. "Quite well, actually."

"How is that possible?" I said. "I thought that only witches and people who had been turned into animals for a time could understand them when they talk."

"That's true," he said. "And when the family curse changed your grandmother, and she sent me to the dungeon, she turned me into a rat for a few days. I've been able to talk to animals ever since. I know every creature in this dungeon, living and dead. It was a centipede who first told me about Hubert. I'm sorry Hubert wasn't very helpful."

"But he was, Grandfather. He gave me just what I needed. Now I know where to go. Can you show us the way to the oubliette?"

"Nasty place," said Grandfather. "Why would you want to go there?"

"Because that's where Hubert died. I think it's time we found his bones."

Five

The oubliette wasn't at all where I thought it might be, so I was glad I'd asked Grandfather to lead us there. Over time, magic had moved doors and holes in the floor so often that even a map wouldn't have helped. When we found it, the metal grate didn't look very sturdy. A lattice of holes as wide as the palm of my hand, it was about three feet square and quite heavy. The grate felt brittle and was hard to move, but Eadric and I were able to lift it free of the opening and set it aside on the floor.

"Now what?" asked Grandfather, floating over the hole as he peered into the darkness below.

"Now I go down there." Taking the piece of string from my purse, I laid it on the floor and made it grow. With a soft hiss, the string stretched until it was longer and thicker. One end of the string fastened to a hook in the wall as the other dropped down into the hole. I listened until I heard the end of the rope slap the floor of the oubliette.

"Let me go first!" said Li'l. She fluttered her wings, circled me once, then swooped into the absolute dark of the hole. "Not much down here," she called. "Just a lot of bones."

"I'll go look," said Grandfather. "Maybe I'll find someone I know." Drifting through the opening, he disappeared from sight.

"I'll go next," said Eadric. "I want to make sure it's safe." Sitting on the edge of the opening, Eadric grasped the rope, hooked one foot around it and slipped down its length. "It seems all right," he called, his voice sounding strangely hollow.

"I'll be right there," I called down and was reaching for the rope when a scrabbling of nails on the stone floor made me stop to listen. At first I thought it was Grassina turned back into a lizard, but when a scrap of shadow detached itself from the gloom, I knew exactly what it was.

"Emma, are you coming?" Eadric called.

"In a minute," I said, stepping back from the edge of the hole.

The glow of my witches' light wasn't very bright, but it was enough to make the shadow moving toward me obvious. The size of a newborn calf, it had no discernable features except for its red eyes. Aunt Grassina had taught me how to deal with the shadow beast years before, so it no longer frightened me as it once had, but

I didn't want it to follow us down into the oubliette where I might not have space to maneuver. Bracing my legs, I waited for it to attack. It came at me in a rush, the scrape of claws on stone its only sound. I waited until the last second, then hit it between the eyes with my fist while I jumped out of the way. Unfortunately my foot caught on the grate that I'd left lying on the floor, and I tripped and fell headfirst into the hole.

"Emma, what are you doing?" Eadric shouted as I plunged toward the floor. Something grazed my hand and I snatched at it, catching the rope and nearly dislocating my arm. The rope swung wildly as I flipped over so I was right side up again. My witches' light bobbed around like a crazy thing, casting shadows that shrank and stretched on the walls and floor like some strange kind of monsters.

I felt Eadric grab my legs. "Let go. I've got you," he said.

Li'l circled me, so close that her wings nearly brushed my face. "Why did you do that?" she asked. "I thought you were going to climb down the rope."

"Are you all right?" Grandfather said, floating up to where I still hung. "Do you need help?" he asked.

"I'm fine," I said, although my voice sounded forced even to me. I took a deep breath. My heart was pounding so hard I was sure everyone could hear it. *Just let go,* I told myself. Unfortunately my fingers weren't listening, and I couldn't make them do anything. "I think I'll stay here awhile," I announced, although my hand hurt and my shoulder shrieked with pain.

"Why?" asked Li'l. "You've almost reached the floor, anyway."

Eadric tightened his grip on my legs. "It's all right, Emma. You aren't going to fall."

"Tell that to my fingers."

"I'll help," said Li'l. Fluttering closer, she nipped my little finger.

"Ow!" I said, more surprised than hurt, and my hand jerked away from the rope. I was relieved when I fell into Eadric's arms.

"Got you!" he said, planting a kiss on my lips. "Now are you glad I came?"

"Yuck!" said Li'l. "Do you have to do that in front of me?"

Eadric laughed. "We're practically engaged, Li'l."

"That doesn't matter. You humans do the strangest things."

"And bats don't?" Eadric asked.

"Not like that!"

"Eadric, put me down," I said. "I have work to do."

"Fine," he said, setting me on my feet. "But you have to admit that I'm handy to have around."

The room was roughly eight feet wide and ten feet long. While one end was dry, I saw gaps in the wall at the other end where stones had shifted, letting water from the moat trickle in. A single skeleton lay sprawled against the driest wall, its legs extending into the middle of the room. However, it was the two corners filled with piles of bones that interested me most. Someone had sorted them neatly, stacking all the skulls in one corner, the rest of the bones in the other. Glancing at the whole skeleton, I decided that he'd probably been the last occupant of the room and the one who'd piled the bones.

"Poor fellow," said Grandfather, hovering above the skeleton. "Even his ghost has abandoned him."

"I don't like this place," said Li'l. "It has a bad feeling. Can we go now?"

"Not until we find what we came for," I said. "Let's start over here." I was picking up an arm bone when a skeletal hand wrapped its fingers around my wrist.

"Not so fast," said a skull in the other pile.

"What do you think you're doing?" asked a second skull.

"Thief! Grave robber!" shrieked a third.

Setting his hand on Ferdy's hilt, Eadric said, "Emma, step back and let me handle this," and drew his sword from his scabbard. Ferdy began to sing.

> I can fight an ogre
> I can fight a troll
> Plain old bones don't....

"That's enough, Eadric," I said. "I can take care of it."

Since skeletons don't have muscles to give them strength, it was easy to pry the bony fingers off my wrist. The hand twitched when I set it on the pile and some finger bones reached up, trying to pinch me while another hand plucked at my sleeve. I sighed and tried not to lose my temper.

The sound of gnashing teeth made me glance up. "All for one and one for all!" hollered a skull with a bad overbite. "Don't let her take a single bone!"

"I don't want any bones," I said. "I just want to borrow a medallion."

"What kind of medallion?" asked a skull with a cracked jaw.

"It's for bravery, and I think it's made of silver. It belonged to Hubert, who worked in Grunwald the third's stables."

"Oh, that medallion!" said a skull.

Another skull grunted. "What do you mean, *that* medallion? There's only one here!"

Something clattered behind me. "Look out!" shouted Li'l, and I turned to see the skeleton clambering to its feet. Tottering on wobbly legs, it raised its arms, its shaking hands reaching for my throat.

"Oh, stop it!" I said and gave the skeleton a shove. It fell against the wall with a thump. Its skull must have been loose, because it fell off and rolled across the floor until it bumped into the opposite wall.

"Serves you right, you big bully!" shouted a skull halfway up the pile.

"You always thought you were special just because you had all your parts!" shouted another on the bottom.

"I never knew you felt that way!" said the skull on the ground. The skeleton patted the stone floor until it located its head, then set it in place on its neck before turning its back to the other skulls.

Putting my hands on my hips, I glared at the skulls and said, "I'm here to do a job, and I'd appreciate it if you'd let me get on with it."

"Maybe we should just leave," said Li'l.

"They won't bother you anymore," said Eadric, scowling at the skulls as if daring them to defy him.

Grandfather floated across the room, his blue outline growing larger and darker until it looked quite menacing. "Perhaps they can help," he said with an edge. "I'm sure they know where we can find the medallion."

"Why should we help you?" asked a wavering voice.

"Because," said my grandfather, "if you don't help, I'll scatter your bones across the kingdom for the wolves and wild dogs to find." The pile of skulls shifted uneasily. "However, if you do help, I'll sort you and see that you get proper burials."

The skulls muttered among themselves until one of

them spoke up. "Do you promise? Cross your rib cage and hope to rest in peace?"

"I promise," Grandfather said solemnly, "on my honor as a king and as a member of the Council of Ghosts."

"Then we'll give the girl the medallion," said the spokes-skull, "but she'll have to return it to its proper owner when she's through with it."

"I'm down here," said a muffled voice that I assumed came from Hubert's skull.

The pile of bones shuddered and heaved. Bones slipped off the top while others were pushed up from the bottom. Finally a bony hand gripping the medallion rose to the surface. Tarnished with age, it was the same medallion that Hubert's ghost had worn on a chain around his neck.

"Thank you," I said, taking the silver disk. "You've been a big help."

"Can we go now?" asked Li'l, flitting around my head.

"You can," I said, "but I won't be going with you." Reaching into my pouch, I took out the bottle of dragon's breath. I had everything I needed now, including a secluded spot from the right century. It wasn't ideal, but I didn't think I'd find anything better.

"What do you mean?" asked Li'l. "You said we could leave as soon as you had what we came for."

"I know I did, and I'm sorry, but I'm going to go learn what I can about the curse. I shouldn't be gone long—not if I do this right."

"Be careful, my dear," said Grandfather. "The past was a harsh and cruel time."

"I will, Grandfather. I'll be back before you know it."

Eadric came to stand beside me and rested his hand on my shoulder. "Don't worry, Your Majesty, I'll keep her safe."

I frowned and shook my head. "I told you, Eadric; you can't go with me."

"And I told you that I am," he replied, looking as serious as I'd ever seen him. "You need me as much as I need you."

"I need you to stay here where it's safe. Who knows what I'll find in the past."

"Exactly," said Eadric.

I didn't want to waste my time arguing, so I shook his hand from my shoulder and edged away, confident that I could move beyond his reach when the spell started to take effect.

Dyspepsia had said that I needed something to enhance my power, but she hadn't said how much I should use. Dragon's breath is very powerful as well as hard to get, so I decided to let out a tiny bit and hope that it was enough. Holding the medallion in one hand, I took the stopper out of the bottle for a moment to let some of the breath escape, then said the spell I'd already decided to use.

> Take me to the day before
> The fairy cast the curse
> That changed my dear aunt's
> temperament
> From kindly to much worse.

I was saying the last line when I heard something scrape against the stones above my head. When I looked up, the glowing eyes of the shadow beast were peering down through the opening.

"Emma!" Grandfather shouted, drifting between the creature and me.

I could hear the shadow beast's nails on the stone floor as it launched itself down into the oubliette. I tried to move out of the way, but the only path open to me was the corner where the pile of bones rested.

"Look out!" screeched Li'l, fluttering around my head.

"Emma, over here!" shouted Eadric. He threw himself at me, pulling me out of the way as the shadow beast lunged, but we were both off balance and we started to fall.

"Careful!" screamed a skull as the whole pile trembled.

Eadric and I were about to land on the pile of bones

when the oubliette disappeared, and we found ourselves rushing down a dark tunnel, propelled by a buffeting wind. A thunderous roar filled my ears, and at first I thought we'd brought the shadow beast with us. When the wind spun me around, I tried to see something, anything in the dark, but my witches' light was gone and I couldn't see a thing. *I hope this is supposed to happen,* I thought as the darkness swept us away.

Six

The air was thickening around me and it was getting harder to breathe. I no longer felt like a wind was whisking me along, but more like something was forcing me through a thick and lumpy, sour-smelling pudding. I could still feel Eadric's arms around me, just as they'd been when he'd pulled me away from the shadow beast. I was frightened, but not nearly as much as I would have been if I'd been alone. Although I hadn't wanted him to come, in a way I was glad he had.

The air grew hotter, and a high-pitched whine filled my ears. I was gasping for breath when something shoved us through a warm, moist layer. Suddenly the air was normal again. We fell—how far I couldn't tell—until we slammed into cold, hard stone, landing on our sides. With the air knocked out of us, we lay sprawled on the ground, too numb to get up.

"What was that?" croaked a voice from somewhere

nearby. "Either I'm dreaming or the rats have gotten a lot bigger."

Wherever we were, we weren't alone. I drew in a ragged breath and was nearly overcome by the stench of dung and an unwashed human body. I tested my limbs, afraid that I might have broken something, but I was fine—aside from scrapes and a few tender spots.

Eadric let go of me and sat up, Ferdy's scabbard scraping the floor. "Are you all right?" he whispered.

"I will be," I said as quietly as I could, "as soon as I find out where and *when* we are."

I was stuffing the medallion and the bottle of dragon's breath into my pouch, when something small and bony landed on me with a Whump! It moaned softly, then started to move around, poking me with knobby edges. "Stupid spell," grumbled a familiar voice.

"Li'l, is that you?" I whispered.

"Emma?" she said. "What happened? One minute I was in that oubliette, and the next thing I knew a wind grabbed me, beat me up and spit me out. Where are we? Did we go back in time?"

"I'm not sure," I whispered. "Shh! Someone's in here, and he thinks he's dreaming."

I set Li'l on my shoulder while I peered into the darkness, hoping for some glimmer of light. I couldn't see a thing until I looked up and saw a swirl of color rising above me—either the dragon's breath or some ghostly apparition that had decided to leave. When it disappeared through a checkered shape that could only be a grate, I knew that we were in the oubliette, although I still had no idea *when*.

I thought about creating a witches' light or using the candle stub so we could see, but if I did, I might have to use more magic to convince the man that he really was dreaming. The longer I thought about it, the more complicated it seemed. No, I'd have to manage without any light at all.

Something shifted in the dark. "Speak up!" said the voice, sounding more like a man and less like a nightmare. "You're awfully quiet for a dream. Why don't you sing me a song? Last dream I had, a minstrel sang about a great knight. Made me feel like I was there, fighting dragons and all. How about a song like that?"

Eadric spoke up, saying, "I'd like to sing, but I don't know any good songs."

"Then I'll sing one," said the voice. "I made it up myself. It's the story of why I'm down here. Want to hear it?" The voice chuckled. "Listen to me—asking a dream what it wants!" He started to sing, scratchy and so far off tune it made me cringe.

> They sent Old Derwin to the pit
> Because he dropped a platter.
> It landed on the good king's crown,

And made an awful clatter.
The king told him to clean it up
As if it didn't matter.
But Princess Hazel threw a fit.
And made the servants scatter.
She said he'd ruined her new gown
Because of what did splatter.
That he was worthless and no good
For anything but chatter.
She sent him down here with no food,
And said he'd get no fatter.
That he was such a clumsy oaf....

"She sent you to the oubliette because you were clumsy? That's horrible!" I said. I'd grown up being ridiculed for my clumsiness, and I thought that had been bad!

"Aye, but the goose gravy made an awful mess. I can't blame the princess for being upset."

"But throwing you into the oubliette—"

"Is that what you call it? I call it the pit."

"And Princess Hazel sent you here?" I asked. If that was true, then the curse must have taken effect already. No one with a shred of kindness in her heart would send anyone to the oubliette. I didn't expect Derwin to have heard the curse firsthand, but nothing stays secret in a castle for long. If people had been discussing it, he might have heard them and....

Derwin sighed. "I should have been more careful," he said. "The princess has been in an awful state what with all those suitors come for her party. Her relatives have come, too, rich and poor alike, and she's trying hard to please them. She's very particular, our princess Hazel, and she deserves the best. Although sending me to the pit does seem a bit harsh, to my way of thinking. I hope they'll let me out when the celebration's over and not just forget about me altogether. It isn't for two more days, though, so I don't expect them anytime soon. Want to hear the rest of my song? Or maybe the one about the milkmaid's dream, since you're part of a dream yourself? It's my longest, so we'll just have to hope that I don't wake up soon."

> A milkmaid dreamed that she could be
> A princess for a day.
> She made a crown of buttercups,
> A throne of fresh-cut hay.

The party hadn't been held yet, although I was earlier than I'd hoped. Now I'd have to stick around for two more days to find out exactly what the fairy had said. Maybe the little bit of dragon's breath I'd used hadn't been enough. I pursed my lips and tried to think, but it wasn't easy with Derwin's singing grating my ears.

"Can't we go now?" Li'l asked, nudging me with her wing. "I don't like it here."

The little bat was right. It was time to go. I'd have to think of some way to get out of the oubliette and go where I could blend in while waiting for the party.

"Just say a spell," said Li'l, "and take us somewhere else."

Engrossed in his song, Derwin didn't seem to hear us, although it wouldn't have made much difference even if he had. We were talking in Li'l's language, and the chances weren't very good that he could understand Bat. "It isn't that simple," I said. "We can't just appear out of nowhere. There's no telling who might be around."

"Isn't that what we just did?" asked Eadric.

"That was different," I said. "Derwin thinks he's dreaming. We don't want anyone else to see us until we're ready. I have to think of a way to get us out of here, but I can't see a thing, so...."

"I can," said Li'l. "I'll show you the way. Although if you were a bat...."

"That's it!" I whispered. "I'll turn us into bats."

"Bats!" said Eadric. "I don't know about that."

"What's wrong?" asked Li'l. "Do you have something against bats?"

"Not at all," Eadric hurried to say. "Bats are very nice."

I don't know why I'd never turned into a bat before.

I'd always admired my little friend's ability to navigate in the dark and hang upside down without getting dizzy. It wouldn't be hard to do, either. After all, it couldn't be much different than turning into a bird, and I'd already done that. Setting Li'l on the floor, I took Eadric's hand and murmured the spell that would get us out of the oubliette, although Derwin was singing so loudly that I doubt he would have noticed even if I'd shouted.

> Silky fur
> And wings of skin
> Change the shape
> That we'll be in.
>
> Neither birds,
> Nor frogs, nor cats,
> We'll now be
> A pair of bats.

Although I couldn't see a thing, I knew when the change was finished because I felt so different. I was smaller, and my body and head were covered with soft fur. Bare skin stretched between my fingers, which had grown long and thin, though my thumb was shorter and could still move freely. The skin between my fingers stretched all the way to my feet, forming wings. More skin connected my tiny feet, and my toes were tipped with long, curved claws.

"Good job!" exclaimed Li'l. "You make a pretty bat, Emma."

"What about me?" Eadric asked.

"You're not bad, either," said Li'l with a lot less enthusiasm.

I glanced up, hoping to see in the dark, but it still looked black as pitch. "Why can't I see? I thought bats could see in the dark."

"We can, but not with our eyes. We make a sound, and it makes a picture in our heads. Try it. You'll see what I mean."

I tried making all kinds of sounds, but nothing unusual happened. Frustrated, I finally made a little sound in my throat, surprising myself when the sound came back, smaller yet quite distinct. A picture of the wall in front of me formed in my mind. *That's funny*, I thought. Turning my head, I made the sound again. When it came back this time, I could tell that the next wall was farther away. *So that's how Li'l does it.* Keeping my mouth open, I made the sound over and over again, until I had a good idea what the oubliette looked like. In this time, there weren't any bones, and the back wall was sturdy and dry.

I'd located Derwin sitting against the wall on the other side of the room, where he was singing with great gusto. When he gestured with his arms, I could see it with my mind, although I still couldn't see anything with my eyes.

I could see Li'l and Eadric, too. "I know what you mean, Li'l," I said. "This is great! Come on, let's get out of here."

"Finally!" exclaimed the little bat.

I tried to move my wings the way I had when I was a bird. My bat wings were very different, however, and it took me a while to get it right. Even then I didn't fly very well. I had to learn new movements while keeping my mouth open so I could make the sounds to see where I was going. It was a lot to master all at once, and I bumbled around the oubliette for a while before it began to feel right. Eadric seemed to have problems, too, although he caught on sooner than I did.

When we finally reached the grate in the ceiling, I was relieved that we fit through the spaces easily. I crawled through one of the holes, still making my sounds, and found that the oubliette was at the end of a short corridor. As we flew away from the grate, I could hear Derwin singing his song, his scratchy voice growing faint with distance.

We reached another corridor, longer than the first and lined on both sides with cells. From the sounds coming through the doors, I could tell that many of them held prisoners. Eadric and I tried to follow Li'l's example, fluttering down the corridor while staying out of the flickering light cast by the occasional torch. This was just as well, for we passed two guards outside the guardroom door and had to make a wide detour around one who'd stopped to relight a torch.

The door at the top of the stairs was closed. We looked carefully, but we couldn't find even the smallest opening through which we could escape. Since there weren't any other ways out of the dungeon, we had to wait until someone opened the door. Li'l chose a point midway between two torches where the shadows were deepest and showed Eadric and me how to cling to the ceiling with the claws on our toes.

My claws held me firmly in place, and I was surprised at how comfortable hanging upside down by my feet could be. It was so comfortable, in fact, that I began to grow drowsy, and I might have fallen asleep if a guard hadn't opened the door at the top of the stairs, letting in a draft that made the torches gutter and rocked us back and forth. The guard was already shutting the door when we zipped past and found ourselves in a dimly lit corridor.

We needed to find someplace private where I could turn us back into humans. The corridor led into a large room smelling strongly of old herbs mixed with bits of rotting refuse strewn over the floor. It was the Great Hall, and it looked much the way it would in my day, just messier. A small group of women talked in a corner while two young men playing chess lounged on a bench nearby. Seeing so many people, Li'l darted toward one of the narrow windows set high in the wall. Eadric and I were following her when a woman shrieked, "Eek, it's a bat!"

"There's a flock of them!" shouted someone else.

Hearing other people behind me, I tried to fly faster and had almost reached the window when a pear sailed past, splatting against the wall and showering me with sticky bits of fruit. They were throwing things at me! I veered away, struggling to keep my balance and saw Eadric dodge someone's thrown shoe.

"It's trying to get in my hair!" shrieked a girl, pulling the end of her surcoat over her head. Other female voices cried out in alarm as they tried to cover their hair as well.

A shoe grazed my back, ruffling my fur. Li'l had already reached the window, but I had to veer off, heading back into the Hall. The women shrieked. I wove back and forth, hoping to dodge anything else they might throw at me as I aimed for the other window. Suddenly the dry straw of an old broom came swishing through the air, knocking me across the room. I tried to right myself, but before I could get my wings sorted out, I landed in a tangle of something limp and greasy.

"It's in my hair!" screamed a voice so close it hurt my ears.

I struggled to free myself until someone started slapping me. Covering my head with my wings, I shut my eyes, curled up into a tight little ball and tried to think of a way out of the mess I was in without using something as conspicuous as magic. If only the woman would stop screaming!

"Got it!" said a triumphant male voice as a hand closed around me, pulling me out of the woman's hair.

My eyes popped open. The florid face of a young man with light brown hair was staring down at me. "Watch this," he said to someone behind him. "I can kill it with one hand!"

My response was automatic, but even if I'd thought about it, I probably would have done the same thing. I bit him squarely on the thumb.

"Aargh!" he shouted, and I was free.

I didn't think I'd bitten him hard enough to do any real damage, although I checked my teeth with my tongue just to make sure. The aftertaste was awful.

Eadric had been trying to reach me, but another young man was chasing him, struggling to trap him in a woven basket. When Eadric saw me, he changed direction and followed me to the window where Li'l was waiting for us on the ledge. Before I followed her into the sunshine, I stopped to look back and was surprised to see that everyone had fled the room. *So much for being inconspicuous,* I thought.

Seven

"Did you have to fool around like that?" asked Li'l. "I thought you were right behind me."

"We were, but those people had other ideas. We need to go outside and…. Oh!" Eadric's jaw dropped as he stared past us out the window.

Even during my short excursion through the castle, I had noticed differences from the way it was in my time. The furniture was sparse, the people's clothing simpler. However, the biggest difference was outside. Unlike our time when flowers were forbidden on the castle grounds, I saw them blooming everywhere. I recognized the roses climbing the walls and growing in massive hedges, having seen the rose-covered cottages at the Old Witches' Retirement Community, but I didn't know the names of most of the rest.

Vines dripping with purple blooms covered the castle. Dark blue flowers nodded at the edge of the moat while small yellow flowers and broad, green pads floated on the water. Trees heavy with pink-and-white blossoms stood like rows of soldiers waiting to be inspected on either side of the road leading away from the drawbridge. Although I didn't know much about such things, it seemed odd that so many plants should bloom at the same time.

"Why would anyone plant flowers around the castle?" asked Eadric. "They make it harder to defend."

I tapped him on the wing and pointed to the other side of the road where hedges of deep pink roses grew in an intricate maze. "That will be perfect," I said, hopping off the ledge.

Li'l and Eadric followed me as I flew to the maze, dodging droning bees and butterflies intoxicated with nectar. "Perfect for what?" Eadric asked.

"For turning back, of course."

"Already?" asked Li'l. "But we were just starting to have fun!"

When we passed the drawbridge, I was shocked to see that vines twined around the chains and threaded through the portcullis. Eadric must have seen it, too, because his wings faltered, and I heard him mutter to himself.

Reaching the maze, we skimmed the rosebushes until I found a secluded niche invisible even to someone looking down from the higher tower. I settled to the ground and used my usual spell to turn us back into humans. No sooner had I smoothed my gown over my hips and adjusted my hem, than I heard voices coming through the maze of shrubs. Eadric heard them, too, and set his hand on Ferdy's hilt, but I shook my head and he took his hand away.

"Why does Millie need a new gown, Mother? It isn't her birthday," someone whined.

Startled, Li'l slipped into a dense section of the hedge where even I couldn't see her.

"I'm sorry, my darling Hazel," a sweet voice replied, "but you want her to look her best for your party, don't you? We wouldn't want her to embarrass you in front of your guests."

"Really, Mother," said a softer voice. "I don't need another gown."

"Nonsense," said Hazel. "Mother is right. You'll get a new gown, but it won't be nearly as nice as mine. Will it, Mother?"

"Of course not, dear. You are the birthday girl, after all."

"And don't forget, Millie," said Hazel as they rounded the hedge, "stay out of my way when … goodness, who are you?" she asked, spotting us for the first time.

Hazel was lovely, but not what I'd expected. She looked like a flower herself, with her porcelain skin, pink cheeks and delicate features. Her thick blond hair reminded me of my mother's. Her lips were the same deep pink as the roses and her eyes a deeper blue than the sky. She didn't look anything like the Green Witch in the tapestry decorating my chamber at home.

The older woman who walked beside Hazel wore a simple gold circlet to secure the veil covering her hair. Shorter than Hazel, she was plump and had worry lines etching her forehead. Her eyes were green, although not as dark as mine, and I could see our family resemblance. However, the face that really surprised me was that of the young girl peeking from behind her shoulder. Except for her dainty, freckled nose and the carrot-red shade of her hair, which was much brighter than my auburn, I might have been looking in a mirror.

"I said, 'Who are you?'" Hazel repeated.

I curtsied and said, "Emma." I wasn't really sure how I should explain my presence since I'd never intended to meet the royal family. I had hoped to talk to one or two people about the curse and leave.

"You must be one of Aunt Frederika's daughters," said Hazel. "There are so many of you; it's hard to keep track."

"Are you settled in, dear?" asked the queen, smiling at me kindly.

"Not really," I said. "I just—"

The queen frowned and shook her head. "Don't tell me that my steward didn't assign you to a room. I'm so sorry. With all our guests, we simply don't…. I know. Millie," she said, turning to the girl behind her, "you have ample space in your chamber. Your cousin can sleep there. I'll have the steward see that a pallet is brought up before supper."

The redheaded girl behind her smiled shyly at me and nodded.

The queen turned to Eadric, who'd been staring at Hazel with obvious admiration. "And you are …?"

Eadric blinked and cleared his throat. "I'm Prince Eadric, a friend of Emma's."

Hazel smiled at him coyly. "Another prince? How nice. Do you come from very far away?"

"Farther than you can imagine," he said. I could have sworn I heard Li'l giggling in the bushes behind us, but no one else seemed to notice.

"Ah," said Hazel. "That explains your unusual clothes. Perhaps one of the other princes could lend you something more becoming. You can share a room with them. We'll have to find a way to fit in one more pallet." She looked me up and down, her eyes lingering on my gown. "Send a tunic and surcoat for her, Mother. That *thing* she's wearing is most peculiar. One of your ladies-in-waiting should have something that would fit her."

"I'm sure we can find her something—" the queen began.

"She is tall, though, isn't she?" Hazel said, brushing

past me on the path. "And I can't imagine where she got that nose."

"We mustn't be unkind to those less fortunate, dear," I heard the queen say as she hurried after her daughter. I could feel the heat rushing to my cheeks, and I knew that I was blushing—something I hadn't done in a very long time. When I glanced at Eadric, he was staring after Hazel with a dazed look in his eyes.

"Don't pay any attention to her," said Millie, patting my shoulder. "My sister is like that with everyone."

"Your sister?" No one had told me that Hazel had a sister, older or younger. It was a shame that so much of our family's history had been lost.

Millie sighed. "I just turned thirteen, so she's only three years older than me, but she acts twenty years older. Come with me. I'll show you where you're going to sleep. I'll have one of the pages take Eadric to meet the princes."

"How many princes are there?" Eadric asked.

"Five," said Millie. "That room is going to be crowded."

I glanced around, hoping to see Li'l, but she must have still been hiding in the bushes. I resolved to come back and find her as soon as I could. "It's awfully kind of you to let me stay in your room," I said, following Millie through the confusing maze.

"Oh, I don't mind," she said. "I'm surprised they

didn't put someone in with me sooner. Mother tends to forget about me, and as for Hazel—well, sometimes I wish she would as well. I shouldn't complain, though. You come from a big family. I suppose it's even worse for you."

"Big family? I don't...." I stopped, remembering that I was supposed to have a whole gaggle of sisters. If my long-ago relatives wanted to believe that I was one of Aunt Frederika's daughters, I wasn't about to try to change their minds.

"The drawbridge is this way," said Millie, leading us between two banks of heavy-headed roses that looked exactly like all the others we'd passed. We had left the maze and were passing the first of the flowering trees when Millie exclaimed, "Oh, look, there are your sisters now!"

Any hope of passing myself off as one of the cousins died the moment I saw them. A cluster of six or seven girls—ranging from a few years older than me to a toddler clinging to her mother's hand—turned to look at us. Like their mother, each one was petite and finely boned; even the oldest girl was fairly short. Although their mother's hair was dark brown, all of the girls' hair was red, but none of them had my high cheekbones or distinctive nose. I wasn't sure what to do, so I waggled my fingers at them in greeting and hurried past, spurred on by their puzzled expressions.

True to her word, Millie called to the first page she saw and had him escort Eadric to the princes' chamber. After that, Millie didn't say another word until we reached her room. Closing her door behind us, she plunked herself down on her narrow bed and turned to me with a determined look in her eyes. "We need to talk," she said, patting the blanket beside her.

I climbed onto the bed. "If it's about Frederika—"

"Don't worry," Millie said. "I understand perfectly. You aren't really one of her daughters, are you? I didn't think you were."

I searched her eyes, hoping she would understand. "When Hazel said—"

"Hazel is wrong more often than she's right, but you'd never get anyone else to admit it." Millie drew her knees up to her chest and hugged them. "You can tell me the truth. I'm very good at keeping secrets."

I shook my head. "You wouldn't believe me if I told you."

"It doesn't matter. I think I already know. Aunt Frederika isn't your mother, but I bet Uncle Markus is your father, and he made his wife take you in and raise you as one of her own. She resents it, doesn't she? The look on her face said it all. Don't worry; it happens in the best of families. I'm right, aren't I?" Millie said, looking very pleased with herself.

"You're too clever for me," I said, delighted that

she'd found her own explanation.

Millie sighed. "Not really. It's just that every family has secrets. Some are easier to figure out than others."

"Don't tell me that you have a secret, too."

Millie turned her head away. Something was troubling her, but I couldn't blame her if she didn't want to tell me about it. After all, we'd only just met. I was about to apologize for being nosy when there was a knock on the door and a pair of chambermaids came in carrying a pallet and an armful of clothes. It didn't take them long to arrange everything to their satisfaction. They were leaving when one of them glanced at my shoes and frowned. As the door was closing, I heard her say to her companion, "Did you see that girl's shoes? They looked like a dog chewed them."

I tucked my feet under me, hoping Millie hadn't heard her. My shoes were scuffed and dirty from tripping in the dungeon, but I didn't think they looked chewed. Certainly none of my father's hounds could have done it, and as for King Grunwald's…. When I thought about it, I hadn't seen a single hound since I'd arrived, although they always seemed to be underfoot in my own time.

"Don't your parents allow dogs in the castle?" I asked.

Millie shook her head. "Not anymore. It's not my parents' idea, though; it's Hazel's. She doesn't like dogs. I suppose she's afraid they'll dig up her precious plants."

"She does have a lot of influence, doesn't she?" I said. I didn't know anyone who could make my father get rid of his favorite hounds.

"Hazel usually gets what she wants. It wasn't always that way, just since she discovered that she could do magic. My parents are afraid of her now, and they do everything they can to make her happy."

I was shocked. The only people in my family who had tried to use magic against a relative had been under the influence of the family curse. The thought that someone might *want* to do it…. "Has she ever used her magic to hurt anyone?"

"Not so far, but she's always dropping hints that she could if she wanted to. Even the threat of withholding her magic is enough to get people to do what she wants. Before she came into her abilities, the kingdom's crops were failing. Hazel turned all that around. I just wish she'd left it at that."

"Then she hasn't actually done anything to anyone?"

"I wouldn't say that. After she figured out that she could do magic, she experimented all the time, and she wasn't always nice about it. She used to have vines tie me up just for fun. Sometimes she'd grow prickly plants on my chamber floor during the night so I'd step on them when I woke up in the morning. She doesn't bother me so much since I learned to stay out of her way and let her think she's getting what she wants."

"But she doesn't always get what she wants, does she?" I asked, seeing a hint of defiance and something I couldn't quite name in Millie's eyes.

"No," she said, a secret smile curving her lips. "Not anymore."

"Doesn't she use her magic for anything productive besides growing crops? What about protecting the kingdom or helping your parents?"

"If only she would! Everyone likes to pretend otherwise, but Greater Greensward is in trouble. Werewolves have been raiding the outlying villages, and I overheard my father talking to his men about vampires. What's even worse is that a dragon has moved into a cave near here. Father sent knights after it, but we never saw them again. He finally stopped sending people, although I know he's been hoping one of Hazel's suitors will kill the dragon for us. It's not going to happen, though. All they want to do is eat our food, drink our wine and flirt with Hazel. Although there is one suitor…."

"What about him?"

"His name is Prince Garrid. He's very handsome if you like men who have wavy, blond hair; deep gray eyes; and cleft chins. He's a good hunter. Every day when the weather is fair he goes off by himself, yet he never fails to come back with some sort of game. Garrid may be the only one who would stand a chance against the dragon. Prince Fenton is said to be good on the jousting field, but that isn't the same as fighting a dragon. What about your friend Prince Eadric? Is he a good hunter?"

"Yes, he is. He's gone hunting with my father many times, and their hunts are always successful. But you shouldn't need to send a hunter after your dragon. Isn't there anyone who could take care of it with magic?"

Millie shook her head. "No one's ever tried, although it wouldn't be a bad idea," she said, getting a faraway look in her eyes.

"So there are werewolves, at least one dragon and who knows what else in the kingdom. Why are your parents still having the party with all this going on?"

Millie shrugged. "It's what Hazel wants and what Hazel wants—"

"Hazel gets!" we said in unison and grinned at each other.

Millie assumed that I was ashamed of my meager possessions and didn't want to fetch them from among Frederika's belongings, so she lent me what I needed, borrowing what she didn't have from others. Once I'd changed my clothes I didn't stand out so much, and I began to relax and enjoy myself. That afternoon Millie showed me around the castle, pointing out her favorite places to hide from her parents and sister. The castle was smaller than in my time, without the entire back section that my great grandfather had added. I acted as if I'd never been there before, oohing and aahing over each of the innovations she pointed out that seemed so old-fashioned to me.

I was amazed when I saw how many flowers had been introduced into the castle, often in inappropriate ways. The larger windows were overgrown with blossoming plants so big they blocked most of the sun, making the castle dark and dismal inside. Climbing the tower stairs, I found the arrow slits filled with blossoms as well, many of which I recognized from their leaves. I'd grown up picking medicinal plants with my aunt Grassina, but had been forbidden to touch them when they bloomed. Finding sweet woodruff, wild thyme, lovage and cowslip growing in the niches that archers used to defend the castle seemed wrong to me. I found sunflowers on the battlements, turning their yellow faces as the sun crossed the sky, while melon vines crisscrossed the stone, forcing me to step carefully. Because of Hazel, the castle was more green than gray, pretty rather than practical.

When we went to supper that night, Millie was careful to keep me away from my supposed parents, telling me how uncomfortable she was sure I must feel around Frederika. Instead of sitting at the high table with her parents and her aunt and uncle, she led me to a table where other young nobles were taking their places. Hazel saw where we were going and abandoned her seat with her parents, scampering off the dais. Smiling gaily at every guest she passed, Princess Hazel shoved her sister aside, taking her seat on the bench beside one of the princes. The trestle tables were arranged in a U with royalty seated at the closed end, so I could see Millie's parents' faces easily. Although King Grunwald didn't seem to notice, the queen—whose name I'd learned was Angelica—watched her daughters flouting protocol with a resigned look on her face, as if she'd seen it all before.

Eadric came in a few minutes later, talking to a young nobleman. He spotted me sitting beside Millie and took a seat on my other side after persuading a sandy-haired prince to move over.

"How are you getting on?" I asked him as pages served the eel-and-prawn stew.

"All right. The room is clean, and the princes seem friendly. That's Prince Fenton over there," he said, indicating the young man beside Hazel. "He follows the tournament circuit and can't resist bragging." He nodded toward the youth with dark hair. "And that's Jasper. He seems nice enough."

When Eadric pointed out Prince Fenton, I recognized him as the leering monster who'd captured me when I was a bat, threatening to kill me with one hand. He seemed affable sitting with Hazel and the visiting princes, but I couldn't keep from shuddering every time I looked his way.

The only other prince who seemed noteworthy was the one Eadric had identified as Jasper. He wore his straight, dark brown hair chin-length like most men of his time. His eyes crinkled when he smiled, and he had an easy, infectious laugh. Even so, I probably wouldn't have noticed him if Millie hadn't spent most of the meal peeking at him, turning away with a guilty start whenever he glanced in our direction. At thirteen, Hazel's little sister was a bit too young for marriage, but not too young to think about it.

"Where is that prince Garrid you mentioned?" I asked Millie, looking down the line of well-dressed nobles for someone fitting his description.

Millie selected a leg of roasted capon from a passing platter and set it on her plate. "He isn't here. On the days he goes hunting, he doesn't come back until after dark. Prince Garrid is the only one of Hazel's suitors who contributes to the table. I think my parents already favor him because of it."

Maybe Eadric should do that, I thought. My mother resented him because he ate so much, but she might not mind his long visits if he provided food on a regular basis.

I was serving myself some beets when two pages bumped into each other, nearly dumping their heaped platters on the floor. It reminded me of Derwin's song about what had happened when he had dropped the platter.

"Millie," I said, "do you know a servant named Derwin?"

"How do you know Derwin?" she asked. "He's one of our oldest servants."

"Have you seen him lately?"

"Hmm," she said, twirling a lock of hair around her finger. "I guess I haven't seen him since the night he dropped the goose on Father. It was kind of funny. Even Father laughed. The only one who didn't was Hazel. She doesn't have much of a sense of humor."

"I heard that she sent Derwin to the oubliette." Maybe I was interfering, but something had to be done.

"I didn't know that! I hope the poor old man is all right. I'll talk to Father about it. There was no call for Derwin to be treated so!"

We were nibbling the final course of cheese and fruit when I overheard some women seated nearby discussing the vicious creature that had attacked them. According to one, a slobbering horror with blazing, red eyes had swooped on them, baring its daggerlike fangs. It took me a while to realize that she was talking about me.

"If it hadn't been for Prince Fenton, we might all have been killed," said one young noblewoman, smiling past her friends to where the prince was helping himself to another slab of venison.

The prince looked down at his thumb wrapped in a strip of clean linen. "Vicious beasts, bats," he said.

I covered my mouth so no one would see my smile, but Jasper must have noticed because he met my eyes and winked. Some of the other princes turned to Fenton and demanded to hear the story.

I was worried about Li'l since we hadn't had a chance to make our plans before Eadric and I had left her. I just hoped she wasn't too frightened alone in the unfamiliar maze. "I need some fresh air," I told Millie. "I'm going for a walk in the garden."

A juggler was strolling past the table, and Millie seemed entranced by the balls he kept circling through the air. "Hmm?" she murmured. "Then I'd better go with you. We're not allowed to walk alone at night."

"But it isn't dark yet," I said, glancing out the window.

Millie gathered her skirts and slipped off the bench. "My father's rules. There are too many dangerous beasts in the area. I told you about the werewolves."

"I can go with Emma," said Eadric, swinging his legs across the bench so he could stand.

"Then you won't need to go, Millie," I said. "Eadric will keep me safe."

Hazel frowned at me. "Perhaps we should all go," she said. Gracing him with her sweetest smile, Hazel took Eadric's arm and led the way. It was almost as if she thought I'd brought her another suitor. I couldn't help feeling a pang of resentment when Eadric bent down to hear what she had to say.

I bit my lip and followed them, trying not to glare at

Eadric and Hazel. I didn't want company. If a group of people went with me, I wouldn't be able to talk to Li'l. I would have said something, except everyone was already heading out the door. Only Jasper dawdled behind as if waiting for me. Hazel glanced back. She made Eadric wait while she held out her hand to Jasper and said, "You may also escort me." Jasper looked my way and shrugged, then linked Hazel's free arm with his.

Millie bumped my elbow. "Look at her," she whispered. "Hazel would have all of them on a tether if she could, and even that probably wouldn't be enough."

The shadows were getting long as we approached the rose-hedge maze, and the scent of the flowers hung heavy in the air. Hazel stepped lightly down the path, surrounded by the princes and a few of the giggling, young noblewomen. Since Millie trailed after Jasper like a lost puppy, it was easier to get away on my own than I'd expected. All I had to do was dawdle until I was left behind, then take an opposite turning once they were out of sight.

The roses were lovely, but after a while they all looked the same to me. I hadn't gone far before I stopped to look around. "Li'l!" I called softly. "Where are you, Li'l?"

It was a little soon for bats to be out hunting, but mosquitoes came out earlier in the shade of the hedge. I could appreciate a good insect, having lived as a frog for a time, but that didn't mean I wanted to feed them. I was slapping my cheek when Li'l fluttered over the top of the hedge and landed on my shoulder.

"Where have you been?" she asked, straightening her wings. "I've been waiting here all day. I can't say that I mind, though. They raise some good, juicy bugs in these shrubs."

When I slapped my neck again and studied the smear of blood and the squashed mosquito on my palm, I noticed that my ring was gone from my hand. I must not be the Green Witch in this time. "So you don't mind staying here for a few days?" I said. "Hazel's younger sister is sharing her room with me, but I don't think she'd understand if a bat joined us."

"I'm fine here. Once you get past the leaves and thorns on the outside, some of these shrubs have nice, cool spaces in their middles. Sit still for a minute and the bugs come right to you. Good place for a nap, too."

"If you're sure you're all right—"

"Sure, I'm sure. It's not as nice as a good cave, but a bat can't have everything."

"I'll try to come see you at least once a day. We have to stay until after the party."

"Fine with me," said Li'l. "I might take a look around, come dark. What's the use of visiting a new time if you can't see the sights?"

"Don't go too far."

Li'l beat her wings and rose into the air. "Don't worry about me. I can take care of myself."

After Li'l left, I retraced my steps, but I guess I'd made more turns than I'd thought. It all looked the same to me, and I might have gotten lost if Millie hadn't shown up. "I took a wrong turn," I said, gesturing back the way I'd come.

Millie gave me a sympathetic smile. "That's easy to do. We have to go now. They'll be raising the drawbridge soon."

I could hear the voices of the others coming through the maze, but there was something else nagging to get my attention. I concentrated and then I had it—the faintest hint of a scent, one that I'd hoped I'd never smell again.

"Hurry," I told Millie, reaching for her hand. "We have to get inside."

A woman screamed, or at least it sounded something like a woman. People in the maze shouted, and I heard the sound of running feet.

Millie tried to pull away from me. "Someone is hurt! We have to go help her."

"No one is hurt," I said, pulling her along behind me as I started for the castle. "That was a harpy. If there's one, there's a whole flock. They rarely travel alone."

"Really?" she said, stopping to look over her shoulder. "I've never seen a harpy."

I tugged on her hand and got her moving again. "Believe me," I said, "you'd be better off if you never did."

I'd seen harpies before. In fact I still had nightmares about them. Foul-smelling creatures with the bodies of vultures and the heads of women, in my time they had taken over a small village in Greater Greensward by chasing away the people who lived there. Once a harpy occupied a house, it took a massive effort to make it clean enough for anyone to live in it again. Harpies smell worse than skunks and leave their odor behind long after they've gone. It had taken me three days and a lot of magic to chase them away, and then the villagers had still refused to come back. If possible, it was better to keep them out in the first place than to have to clean up their mess afterward.

I was pulling Millie onto the drawbridge when the first harpy appeared. Shrieking wordlessly, it swooped down on us. I would have used my magic to turn the creature away, except I didn't want anyone to know that I was a witch. When I threw up my hands to ward it off, a boy dressed like a stable hand shouted and came running with a stout staff. Waving the staff in the air, he forced the screeching harpy higher. We were almost beneath the portcullis when the creature began pelting us with dung. It missed Millie and me, but hit the boy squarely on the back. It would have hit him again if he hadn't kept running.

Once we were inside, Millie and I thanked him profusely. After he ran off to the stable, Millie said, "That boy saved us from a stinky fate. I think he deserves a reward."

Although he looked very different from his ghost, the shape of his nose and the jut of his chin were similar enough that I'd recognized him. It was Hubert. "I think so, too," I said. "In fact I think he deserves a medal."

❧

Eadric had been with Hazel and her friends when the harpies attacked. According to Hazel, nearly a dozen harpies had pelted them with sticks and clods of dirt. Eadric was the only one carrying a sword, and he'd made a real impression with his skill and bravery. I heard all about it after they reached the castle. Hazel's voice was almost as loud as the harpies' by the time she joined us.

The entire castle was in turmoil as soldiers ran to defend the gates and the battlements, servants rushed to fetch water from the castle well to heat for baths and everyone else ran around, shouting questions that no one seemed able to answer. We found the queen in the Great Hall, wringing her hands. "What a time for this to happen!" she wailed. "We have a castle full of guests and more on the way!"

"Where is Father?" Millie asked, trying to get her mother's attention. "I have to see him."

The queen grabbed her daughter by the arm and held on tightly. "Oh, no you don't, young lady. You'll just get in the way! You're staying here with me until this is over."

Although I understood how frustrated Millie must feel, her mother's interference helped me. I needed to go somewhere without anyone following me or suspecting that I had gone. Afraid that the queen might try to make me stay as well, I slipped into the milling crowd and headed for the stairs that led to the unfinished tower.

The stones were thick with dust and the door leading to the tower was jammed, but when I finally forced it open I had the ideal vantage point. Soldiers stationed on the battlements across from where I watched thrust their swords at the harpies, who flew just out of reach, pelting them with dung. Although archers shot one volley after another at the bird women, only a few found their mark. A group of harpies was concentrating on the battlements just above the gate, but there were so many of them that I found it hard to see why, until a harpy fell and I spotted the king surrounded by his knights. A sword flashed and another harpy fell, making the rest of the creatures draw back. The knights moved as a group, trying to escort the king to the only completed tower and safety.

Although I remembered Dyspepsia's warning about

not changing the past, I had to interfere. It may not have been my time but it was my home, and I couldn't stand to see it taken over by harpies. While everyone watched the monstrous creatures, I hid in the tower doorway to recite the spell I had in mind. I knew how persistent harpies could be, so I had the spell cover their return just in case.

Oh, ye wind of far-flung places,
Keep these harpies from this home.
Should they force themselves upon us,
Blow them all from here to Rome.

At first it was a light breeze caressing my cheek and lifting the hair that had come loose from my braid. Within seconds it was a wind strong enough to blow a man's cap from his head. In less than a minute, I had to fight to get back into the tower room. The harpies flying over the battlements were carried off while I strained to shut the door. From the sound of their screaming, the rest of the harpies soon followed them.

When I rejoined the crowd in the Great Hall, the king and queen were standing near the high table, talking in muted voices. They looked up at the approach of one of their knights.

"Your Majesties," said the knight, "the harpies have gone."

"But how? Why?" asked the king.

"It was the wind, sire. It carried them away."

"Wind? You're making no sense, man. There is no wind today."

"It started suddenly, sire, and it's already stopped."

"You don't suppose it was magic, do you?" asked Queen Angelica.

The king nodded. "It must have been."

"Then it had to have been Hazel's doing."

"Where is the girl?" asked the king. "I wish to talk to her."

"She's locked herself in her chamber," said one of the young ladies who had followed the princess into the maze, "and she refuses to come out."

"Then she performed the magic from there," said the king. "I must thank her."

"I don't know what we would have done without that darling girl!" the queen gushed.

"Let's go," Millie whispered, coming up behind me. "If I have to listen to any more of this, I'm going to be sick."

I followed Millie up the stairs to her chamber. We got ready for bed and Millie went to say good night to her parents. When she came back, she told me that Hazel had kept her door locked, refusing to come out until her parents had assured her that the harpies were gone. "She'd blocked her windows with climbing roses," said

Millie. "Their perfume was so strong it gave everyone else a headache. My father no longer thinks that she was the one who got rid of the harpies."

"Really?" I said, trying to sound surprised. "Then who does he think it was?"

"That's just it," said Millie. "No one knows. Maybe it was one of the princes. We don't know much about them. That's what I wanted to discuss with you. I hate to ask you for a favor since you're a guest, but I need your help."

"What do you need me to do?" I asked.

"Hazel is supposed to announce the name of the suitor she's chosen at the party. When we went for our walk, she was discussing Fenton's tournament wins with him, so she didn't hear the other princes, but I did. They didn't say anything wrong exactly, and I know they were joking, but they said some things that made me wonder why they're asking for her hand. Is there even one among them who loves her? I'd feel better if we could find out what they really want."

"I'll talk to Eadric. Since he's sharing a room with the princes, maybe he can learn more about them."

Millie sighed. "Thanks. At least that's a start." Her bed creaked as she turned over.

I lay awake thinking, long after Millie's breathing became soft and even. She was a sweet girl, and we'd taken to each other right away. She was also a relative, although a distant one. If she needed my help, I would try my best.

As I lay in bed, wishing I could fall asleep, it occurred to me that there might be something more I could do than just find out what the curse had been after it happened. Maybe I could do something about the curse itself. Maybe I could keep it from being cast. I already knew that Hazel had offended the fairy by failing to give her an everlasting bouquet. It shouldn't be hard to make sure that didn't happen. She'd just have to make more bouquets—enough to give one to everyone, including every fairy. If I ended the curse before it began, Grandmother and Grassina would never have turned nasty, Grandfather wouldn't have died in the dungeon, Grassina could have married Haywood and I could marry Eadric. It sounded like the perfect solution to everyone's problems. I remembered Dyspepsia's warning about the dangers of altering history, but it wasn't hard to convince myself that the kind of change I had in mind couldn't hurt anyone. Believing that I'd just had the best idea yet, I drifted off to sleep, worry free for the first time in months.

Eight

When we went downstairs the next morning, the Great Hall was empty except for some pages polishing swords. I had hoped to catch a glimpse of the elusive prince Garrid, but when I asked one of the pages where I might find him, I was told that the prince had already gone hunting.

Breakfast in the castle was haphazard, since most people preferred to wait for dinner at noon. Millie and I were hungry, however, so we collected bowls of porridge from the kitchen. We had just finished eating when Queen Angelica took Millie off to see to her new gown. Left on my own, I went in search of Hazel, prepared to do whatever it took to make sure she was ready for all the guests at her party. I finally ran into her when she was leaving her mother's chamber. She barely glanced at me as she swept past.

"Hazel," I said, hurrying after her. "I've been meaning to ask you how the preparations are coming for your party."

She turned to look at me, curling her lip in a way that reminded me of my mother. "Ask the castle steward. I have better things to do with my time."

"I just meant that I'd be happy to help," I said as she started to turn away.

She looked me up and down, and said, "What could you possibly do?"

"Help with the decorations, I suppose. Or perhaps the gifts for the guests."

"Gifts for the guests?" she said, frowning ever so slightly. "I have thought about giving them something. I'll decorate with flowers, of course, and I daresay I'll give out flowers as well. I'm known for my green thumb, you see," she said, holding up her left hand. Her thumb was actually green, the same shade of green as the skin of some wood nymphs I'd seen. I wondered if the blood of a wood nymph flowed in her veins. "People come to me from all the kingdoms around when they need help with their crops. Giving them flowers, an everlasting bouquet perhaps, would remind them of how much they need me."

"I'm sure everyone will love them. How many do you plan to make?"

"Why does that concern you?"

"I just want to help, that's all. It would probably be a good idea to make extras. You never know how many guests will show up at the last minute."

"You don't have to worry. I'm sure there will be enough for you to have one, too."

"That isn't what I meant—"

"Greedy thing, isn't she?" Hazel said to one of her mother's ladies-in-waiting. "But then the poorer relatives often are." She sneered at me, then tossed her head and walked away.

I tried not to let her attitude bother me. It wasn't so much the way she treated me as the knowledge that this girl was my ancestor. I'd always wanted to believe that my ancestors were better people than they probably really were.

After talking to Hazel, I needed to see a friendly face. Millie was still busy with her mother and I couldn't find Eadric anywhere, so I decided to go outside to visit Li'l. Except for the droning of the bees, the maze was quiet when I reached it. Li'l didn't come right away when I called her, and I was beginning to wonder if something had happened to her when she finally showed up.

Landing on a full-blown rose that bent double under her weight, Li'l opened her mouth to yawn, then said, "What's up?"

"I'm sorry I woke you. I wanted to know about your night. You said you might go exploring."

The little bat shifted her feet like she does when she's excited. "It was great! I went to the forest. It's bigger now than in our time. There are fewer farms between here and there and a lot more places for a bat to live. Lots of bugs, too. I was chasing a firefly when I met him."

"You met a bug?"

"Course not! Just the handsomest bat I've ever seen. He was chasing the same firefly, but he let me have it. A real gentlebat, that's what he was. I wish you could meet him. You'd like him; I'm sure of it."

I had to smile. "A gentlebat, you say. How nice."

"He showed me around. We saw the waterfall where the wood nymphs wash their hair and the ring where the fairies dance. We missed the early show, and the musicians were taking a break when we got there, so we waited for them to come back. The dancers were so graceful and light on their feet."

"They have wings, don't they?"

"That's true. Anyway I didn't get back until it was almost dawn. Bugsy brought me home."

"Bugsy?"

Li'l ducked her head as if she was embarrassed. "That's what I called him, and he didn't seem to mind. He's so good at catching bugs."

"Hmm," I said, watching my little friend preen her wings, something I'd never seen her do before. "Do you think you'll see him again?"

Li'l bobbed her head. "He's coming back tonight. We're watching the unicorn races in the Silver Glade and going out for beetles afterward."

"Then you'd better get your rest," I said. "It sounds like you're going to need it."

It was still early, so I went for a walk around the castle, admiring the variety of flowers that grew at the edge of the moat. After a while I heard the distant clang of metal on metal. The sound grew louder as I approached the practice field where the princes were showing their sword-fighting techniques to a group of squires not much younger than themselves. Jasper was correcting a squire's stance when he looked up and saw me. He smiled and waved before turning back to his pupil.

I noticed Eadric at the same time that he noticed me. Excusing himself from his companions, he joined me in my walk. "Millie wants to know more about the princes," I said. "It would help if you could keep your eyes and ears open and find out what you can."

Eadric laughed. "That won't be a problem. You learn a lot about people when there are six of you crowded into one little room. I already know who snores and who doesn't like to wash. And Garrid must be having some sort of intestinal trouble."

"You mean you've met him?"

Eadric nodded. "He came in late last night and left the room a short time later. We were all asleep, but my pallet is so close to the door it wakes me every time someone leaves the room. Poor guy didn't come back until it was almost dawn."

"Maybe it was something he ate," I said.

"Maybe," said Eadric. "Say, you should see some of the birthday gifts the princes have brought for Hazel. Jasper has this cup…."

"I forgot about the gift! We have to get her one!"

"At the magic marketplace?" asked Eadric.

"We don't have time for that. We'll have to make it."

Eadric rubbed his jaw. "I suppose I could find some wood and carve a buckle…."

"Never mind," I said, rolling my eyes. "I'll think of something."

"Tell me," he said. "Why have you been making faces at me ever since we got here? You look as if you're angry half the time."

"I haven't been making faces! I'm just not happy about the way you've been acting."

"What do you mean?" Eadric said, scowling. "I've been doing my best to fit in. I helped fight off the harpies and have spent most of my free time giving lessons to the squires. What more do you want from me?"

"That's wonderful, but it's not what I'm talking about. It's the way you hang on everything Hazel says and let her whisper in your ear. You really like her, don't you?"

"Hazel? You've got to be joking!" said Eadric. "Sure, she's pretty, but she has as much substance as one of your cook's pastries and isn't nearly as sweet. The girl doesn't think of anything except herself. Do you know she wanted me to sit at her feet singing songs about her beauty when I'd already promised the squires I'd show them how to track werewolves? I had to lie and say I couldn't carry a tune before she'd leave me alone."

"You mean you can sing?"

"Sure, when I have to. So, that's what this is all about? You think I've been paying too much attention to Hazel?"

"You don't seem to mind the way she flatters you and touches your arm or your hand."

"I'm trying to fit in, remember? Watch Fenton, or any of the other princes, and see how they act around her. I don't spend nearly as much time with Hazel as they do."

"But they're her suitors. You're supposed to be mine!"

"And I am," he said, pulling me into his arms.

❧

The royal family was sitting down to dinner when we returned to the castle. I took a seat between Eadric and Millie again, with Hazel on Eadric's other side. Hazel made a big show of praising Eadric for fending off the harpies, and I noticed that she felt the muscles in his arms more than once. I ground my teeth and didn't say anything, even when Hazel took morsels off her plate and put them on his. But when she offered to show him the gardens, I couldn't keep from telling her, "He's already seen them with me."

Hazel sneered. "It wouldn't be the same, Emma dear. I know all the gardens' secrets. I could show him things he's never seen before."

"I just bet you could," I muttered into my mug of cider.

An elderly servant carried a platter the length of the table, offering everyone a slice of boiled mutton. "Derwin looks well now, doesn't he?" Millie said to me, using her knife to point out the elderly man. "I had them give him a bath when they pulled him out of the oubliette. I think it was the only bath he's ever had."

"Thank you," I said. "I'm sure everyone here appreciates your thoughtfulness."

I was listening to Millie describe her new gown when there was a commotion at the far end of the Hall. One of the king's foresters was trying to get past a guard who seemed determined to keep him from entering.

"You can't see him now," said the soldier.

"It's an emergency, I tell you," said the forester. "King Grunwald needs to hear about this."

"About what?" asked the king from the raised dais.

"The dragon is back, Your Highness. He's been spotted carrying off a prize bull. We think he ate the farmer."

King Grunwald set down the drumstick he'd been gnawing and rose to his feet. "I need volunteers," he said, looking directly at the row of princes. "Some brave young men skilled in fighting who aren't afraid to take on a dragon. Who among you is man enough to kill the foul beast?"

One prince looked away as if meeting the king's eyes would commit him to going. Another pretended to be busy with his food, acting as if he hadn't heard a word the king had said. Only a few young men stood, Eadric, Fenton and Jasper among them.

"I'll go, sire," said Eadric. "I need the practice."

Fenton made a rude sound, then said, "I'll go, sire, to prove I'm worthy of Princess Hazel's hand."

"I'll go, sire," said Jasper, "to rid the countryside of a terrible scourge."

"I'll go, sire," said two knights.

"For honor," said one.

"For glory," said another.

"For goodness' sake," I whispered to Millie. "Do they all have to be so dramatic?"

"Perhaps they are braver than I thought," murmured Millie. "Imagine, killing a dragon!"

"They haven't fought it yet. I think we should reserve judgment until we see what they actually do."

"But those brave young men are going to risk their lives!"

"Maybe," I said, reaching for a piece of bread. I was torn in a way. I had friends back home who were dragons, so I knew they weren't all bad, but having a dragon live so close to the castle was bound to cause trouble. While I didn't want to see the dragon get hurt, I didn't want to see any of the princes get hurt, either, especially Eadric. But then they wouldn't have to fight at all if I could help it.

After dinner Eadric and the other princes left the Great Hall to collect their horses and weapons. I slipped away from Millie while she was talking to her parents and made my way to the garden. I'd thought about discussing my plans with Eadric, but he'd insist on going without me and handling it on his own, and that was the last thing I wanted.

Although Eadric was the bravest man I knew, he was more likely to wave his sword, Ferdy, in the dragon's face than he was to talk to him. Even after we'd become friends with a nice family of dragons, Eadric believed that they were the exception, and that most dragons were horrible monsters that deserved to be slain. We'd argued about it many times, but neither of us was willing to give in.

Once again I remembered Dyspepsia's warning, but since I'd already interfered when I chased away the harpies, I didn't think that getting rid of a dragon would be so bad. It wasn't like I'd be killing anyone. If all went well, I'd be saving lives, although I'd have to hurry to do it. If no one, human or dragon, was to get hurt, I'd have to be the one to confront the beast first. I was a witch and could use my magic if necessary. I also had a special salve with me that would protect me from the dragon's flames. Even more important, I was a Dragon Friend. In a tent at the Dragon Olympics, I'd been given the title after passing a test that could have taken away my magical powers. I hadn't had any need to verify it before, but I hoped the dragons had told me the truth when they said that the title would earn me the respect of dragonkind everywhere.

Wanting to be as inconspicuous as possible, I hid in a secluded spot in the maze and took out my farseeing ball, focusing it on all the places around the kingdom where I thought a dragon might lurk. A farseeing ball is a handy thing to have, although it does have its limitations. You can use it to keep an eye on someone who has recently touched it or to see places that you have visited. Getting it to do anything else isn't easy.

I decided to look where I had seen dragons in my own time. When I focused on the enchanted forest, I saw griffins skimming the treetops and unicorns butting heads, but no dragons. There were water sprites splashing in a stream, fairies dozing under flower petals and werewolf pups wrestling, but no dragons.

"Hmm," I said, and turned my attention to the

Purple Mountains. Deep in a cave where the Dragon King would one day keep his treasures, I saw nothing except bats hanging by their toes in the dark. I looked at a huge, high-sided arena, where the dragons would hold their Olympics in the future. There were no dragons yet.

When Eadric and I had been looking for a green dragon, I hadn't had enough experience or power to use a spell to find one. Now it was almost as easy as breathing. Cupping the farseeing ball in my hands, I said:

Sharp of tooth and fierce of claw,
With a gaping, hungry maw,
Find the dragon close to here,
Make the image very clear.
Show the path that I must take
To reach the beast; there's much at stake.

An image of a dragon took shape in the farseeing ball. Asleep in a cave, the dragon moved restlessly as it dreamed. There wasn't enough light to see its color or anything to compare it to that would indicate its size. While I watched, the image changed, pulling away from the dragon and leaving the cave. I saw a steep-sided ravine, a wooded slope and a path trampled flat by feet with claws long enough to gouge the ground. The path led through the forest until it dwindled away among the trees. The image continued however, showing me a break in the trees here, a deer trail there, until it met a road rutted by cart wheels. The image in the farseeing ball moved faster now, following the road where it passed between the trees and through farmers' fields, becoming wider and hard packed when it met another road. I recognized the area now; the slope of the hill and the outcropping of rocks hadn't changed much in a few hundred years.

As the image dissolved, I recited the spell to turn myself into a dove. It took just a moment, but even so, the first of the princes had appeared by the time that I was ready to go. Wearing a dented but serviceable suit of armor, Prince Jasper rode an older destrier, a huge warhorse bred for carrying the weight of a man clad in metal. What little I could see of the horse was golden brown. It, too, wore plain, undecorated armor and moved with a steady and purposeful gait.

I took to the air just as Prince Fenton arrived astride a more highly spirited horse that pranced rather than walked. Solid black, the horse wore armor that matched the prince's. Both sets were decorated with twin lions and an eagle and were so highly polished that it hurt my eyes to look at them.

I darted past Prince Jasper, following the road and leaving the armor-clad horses stirring up dust behind me. Anxious to deal with the dragon before the princes arrived, I flew as fast as I could and was exhausted before I reached the forest. The first tree I saw was an ancient oak, and I stopped to rest on one of its lower branches to let my pounding heart slow to a steadier pace. I took off again when I heard the clanking of the horses' armor and wondered how the princes ever thought they could catch a dragon unaware.

I found the deer trail right away and was approaching the break in the trees when I heard something snuffling. Wary, I slowed my pace and veered away from the trail while trying to keep it in sight. When I saw what was making the sound, I was glad I hadn't blundered ahead. A griffin as big as a small dragon stood over the carcass of a wild boar, tearing at the animal's hide with its wickedly curving beak. The griffin's wings were splattered with drops of blood and its lionlike sides heaved from exertion, but it wasn't too tired to look up when I flew through the far side of the clearing. Reaching the trees, I tried to put as much distance as possible between the eagle-eyed creature and myself. I was convinced that I was about to be plucked from the air, so I flew farther than I'd intended and didn't slow down until I nearly flew into a thorn-covered thicket. As I slowed my pace, I realized two things: the griffin wasn't following me, and I was lost.

It took me a while to get my bearings and locate the dragon's path. I wouldn't have found it at all if I hadn't stumbled across a charred tree trunk. There was another beyond it, and after that most of the trunks were scorched and scarred. Great furrows rent the ground as if huge creatures had scuffled there in the past, and a few pieces of partly melted armor told me that at least one of the battles had been between dragon and knight.

The damage grew more extensive as I continued on until the trees gave way to a gully twice as deep and three times as wide as a man is tall. I could see the opening of the dragon's cave on the far side of the gully. Unfortunately King Grunwald's forester must have been able to give good directions, because Jasper and Fenton had arrived as well. They sat astride their horses at the edge of the burned trees, their armor smudged with soot, looking down at the opening of the cave. While I was relieved that Eadric wasn't there, I hoped he hadn't gotten lost.

Jasper's horse stood his ground, but Fenton's steed was skittery, dancing aside and refusing to go on. When Fenton tried to urge him forward, the horse dug in his heels and threw up his head, rearing each time the prince yanked on the reins. "Blasted horse," muttered Fenton. Finally, with stiff movements and a lot of effort, Fenton backed his horse away from the gully and struggled to climb off.

I landed on the blackened branch of a nearby tree. Although it was too late to talk to the dragon before the princes arrived, I could still make sure that no one got hurt.

I'd been watching Fenton, so I hadn't noticed that Jasper had already dismounted and tied his horse's reins to a branch. "Come out, you cowardly worm!" Jasper shouted, and I turned to see him wielding his sword and shield at the edge of the ravine.

There was a strange whuffing sound from the cave, and a puff of pink smoke curled from the entrance.

"I'm not ready yet, Jasper!" yelled Fenton, still only halfway off his horse. "Wait for me! I just—"

A roar from the gully nearly knocked me from my perch. Fenton's horse took off, galloping through the forest with his master draped over his side, fighting to stay on. I saw Jasper step back a pace, then raise his sword above his head. Flying higher into the tree, I looked down into the gully. Scorching flame had burned away every twig and scrap of foliage, giving me an unimpeded view of the massive head that emerged a moment later.

I had seen many dragons before, and some of them bore scales as beautiful as precious gems, yet this dragon's scales were a particularly ugly color. A muddy, washed-out yellow, he looked even worse when he scuttled from his cave into the sunlight and raised his head to glare at Jasper. The dragon was smallish, with a patchy look, missing or damaged scales, and ragged wings. His legs were stiff when he ran, as if his joints hurt. He opened his mouth, and I saw that his teeth were crooked;

he was missing more than a few.

When the dragon sucked in air through his gaping mouth and pulled his wings back to his sides, I knew that he was about to flame. Without shield or armor to protect myself, I leapt into the air, rising high above the gully.

Holding his shield in front of his face, Jasper jumped to the side as the flame licked the ground at his feet. Although deadly, the flame wasn't very long and it dwindled at the end to a meager trickle of fire. My dragon friend, Grumble Belly, would have been embarrassed to call it his.

"Hold on!" shouted Fenton from the forest. "I'm coming! Dratted horse wouldn't stop!"

Seeing the prince still on his feet, the dragon started up the side of the gully, huffing pink steam as he ran with a shambling sort of gait. Jasper darted behind the closest tree as quickly as his armor would let him. I thought he was running away until he stopped and raised his sword. The trunk was singed nearly to the heartwood, the tree obviously dead, but since it was broad at the base and still standing, it made a fairly good shield.

The clank of metal came through the trees. "I'm almost there!" shouted Fenton, sounding out of breath even from a distance.

The dragon snorted, and flame curled from his nostrils.

"Come on, worm," taunted Jasper. "Is that all you can do?"

Even as he ran, I could hear the dragon sucking air into his lungs, and he began flaming while he was still too far to reach the tree. Shield up, Jasper crouched behind the trunk. The moment the dragon's flame shrank and died, the prince sprang to his feet and ran around the trunk, his sword aimed at the muddy-yellow head.

"Here I am!" shouted Fenton as he emerged panting from the trees, his sword and shield dangling uselessly from his hands.

Jerking his head up, the dragon spun around to face Fenton, his long tail whipping behind him. As Jasper ran at the dragon, the tail hit him with a clang, sending him sailing through the air. The prince hit the ground, his body rolling a few feet before lying motionless.

"Uh-oh," said Fenton, when the dragon lunged in his direction, his ribs expanding as he inhaled again.

The first hint of flame was just leaving the dragon's mouth when Fenton turned and ran. For a moment he looked like a shiny blur disappearing into the dark of the forest—and then he was gone.

Without an enemy to incinerate, the dragon's fire died down to a fizzling puff. He turned with a grumble and started back toward Jasper, whose body still lay where it had fallen. Alarmed, I flew lower to see what I could do. Jasper was defenseless; if he was alive, he wouldn't be for long. *This isn't right,* I thought. It was time for me to intervene.

As the dragon lowered its massive head to snuffle the injured knight, I darted down and pecked the creature on the back of his skull. The beast didn't notice me. Opening his jaws, he grasped an armor-clad leg and began to drag Jasper toward the edge of the gully. I tried to think of some magic spell I could use that wouldn't hurt either combatant, but then the dragon's ear flopped over. In the blink of a unicorn's eye, I darted toward the ear and pecked just inside its leathery opening. The dragon jerked his head up in alarm, dropping Jasper. I clung to his scales with my claws as he threw his head from side to side. When he calmed down again, I pecked once more to make sure I had his attention, then let go of his scales and took off. Since I didn't want him to lose sight of me, I stayed low to the ground, zigzagging so he wouldn't hit me if he flamed. The dragon roared and came after me, which was just what I wanted. I planned to lead him into the woods, then come back for Jasper, but someone else had different plans.

Both the dragon and I heard her voice at the same time. A girl was down in the gully, whimpering and calling out and making herself an irresistible target for an angry dragon. I tried to distract the beast, but the possibility of an easy meal was too tempting to ignore. When he scrambled down the steep slope, I flew past him and

127

gasped. It was Millie, looking small and vulnerable in the burnt-out gully. At first sight of the dragon, she threw up her hand and pointed, a familiar gesture, but not one I would have expected her to use. Her voice rang out loud and clear as she recited a spell she must have made up herself.

> Dragon, dragon in my sight,
> You don't always have to fight.
> Turn around and go back home.
> Never more to want to roam.

I wasn't surprised when the dragon started spinning in circles since the spell had told him to turn around, although Millie's mouth dropped open and her eyes grew wide. I wondered how long it would take her to realize that she was standing between the dragon and the cave he currently considered his home, the very place she had just sent him. I was more surprised that Millie was a witch, although I really shouldn't have been. After all, she was a distant relative, and just because her sister had the talent didn't mean that it wouldn't show up in her as well.

I watched the dragon spin, moving one step closer to his cave each time he turned around. At that rate, it would take him ten minutes to reach the opening, giving me plenty of time.

I'd been circling in the sky over the gully, but now

that I'd made up my mind, I changed the angle of my wings and fluttered down to land beside Jasper. He was trying to get up, a difficult task for anyone wearing a suit of armor. From the way he was moving, I could tell that he was going to be all right. I would have stayed and tried to think of a way to help him without giving myself away, but I heard a shriek from down by the cave and knew that I had to hurry.

After making sure that Jasper couldn't see me and that the other princes were nowhere around, I said the spell that would turn me back into my human self and hurried to the edge of the gully. The dragon must have gone faster once he realized what was happening, because he had almost reached the cave. As the dragon spun nearer, Millie covered her mouth with her hand, stifling a scream. She had the look of a cat I'd once owned that had been too frightened to move when a dog came after her. I'd had to step in then, just as I'd have to step in now. The dragon was close enough that even his meager flame would engulf her.

I no longer cared if Millie saw me use magic because we shared a common secret. Pointing my finger at the dragon, I said a quick and easy binding spell. The dragon stopped in midspin, his mouth gaping as if he was about to flame. Hurrying down the slope of the gully, I shouted to Millie, "Go home! I'll handle this now."

"Emma, you're a witch!" Millie declared as if telling

me something I didn't know.

"And so are you, but I have more experience with dragons, so let me handle this. There is something you can do, though. Jasper needs your help getting back to the castle." I pointed up the slope. "You'll need to help him to his feet, then onto his horse."

"Jasper needs me?" Millie said, a faint blush coloring her cheeks. "I'd better go. Are you sure you'll be all right?"

"I'll be fine. Go help the prince," I said. "That's where you'll do the most good. By the way, do you have any idea what happened to Eadric?"

"I remembered what you'd said about using magic to protect the kingdom. I think it's a wonderful idea, but I didn't want anyone else around when I tried it on a dragon. When I saw Eadric and some of my father's knights starting out, I used a little magic to send them in the wrong direction. I would have sent Jasper and Fenton the wrong way, too, if they hadn't already left the castle."

"Good thinking, Millie," I said. "Any more men clanking around in suits of armor, and we might have had a real problem keeping this a secret. And we will keep the fact that we're both witches a secret, won't we?"

Millie nodded, and I thought she looked relieved. While I waited for her to climb out of the gully, I opened my pouch and found the vial Ralf had given me. Ralf was a young dragon who had become one of my best friends. Shortly after we met, he had taken Eadric and me to the Dragon Olympics and given us some salve to protect us from dragon flames. It was the same salve used on baby dragons until their sensitive skin became tougher. The salve had worked perfectly, so I was happy to accept when he offered to give me some to keep on hand just in case.

It didn't take much salve to cover my face and hands, but I went further than that, wiping it on my clothes and in my hair, on my neck and even on my eyelids. It made me feel greasy and disgusting, but at least it smelled nice, kind of like peppermint. Since I'd used most of the vial, I'd have to ask Ralf for more as soon as I got home.

When I thought I was ready, I tapped the dragon on his back and hurried out of the way. Even wearing the salve, I didn't want to stand too close.

"Hrumph!" grunted the dragon, shaking his head. Smoke billowed from his mouth as he looked about for his prey. "Where'd it go?" The dragon turned a half circle before spotting me. "A different one," he said, "but it should be just as tasty."

"Wait!" I said, but the dragon had already built up a good fire in his belly and was eager to use it. I shut my eyes as the flames washed over me. It felt hot, but no hotter than the sunshine on a summer's day. When it grew feeble and finally stopped, I opened my eyes and looked down. I looked wet and shiny from the salve, although the flames hadn't done a thing.

The dragon looked at me in surprise. "What happened?" he said. "It should be crispy. And that smell…." He took a step toward me and sniffed. His gaze softened and he almost seemed to be smiling. "That smells like the salve my mother used when I was just a hatchling. How did a human get hold of it?"

"It is the same salve," I said. "A friend gave it to me."

"It knows the true tongue!" the dragon exclaimed, flicking his ears in agitation. "I didn't know humans were able to speak it."

"I'm a witch. I can do a lot of things most people can't."

"Why haven't I seen you before, human?" he asked, his eyes narrowing.

I didn't want to let him know that I was there for only a short time. If my plan worked and he left, I wouldn't want him to think he could come back. "I've been away," I said. "And I have a name. I'm Princess Emeralda, the Green Witch."

"Green Witch, you say? I've never heard of you."

"How could you, if you don't speak human?"

"You have a point," said the dragon, sitting back on his haunches. "Who was this friend who gave you the salve?"

"A young dragon named Ralf," I said.

"So what do you want with me?"

"I want you to move away from here. Find some-place to live where there aren't any humans around."

The dragon snorted a puff of pink smoke that smelled like boiling cabbage. "Why should I?" he said. "I like it here."

"Because I told you to and I'm the Green Witch, which means that it's my duty to protect the kingdom. If you stay here, I'll have to do something neither of us will like."

The dragon drew his brows together in a fearsome scowl. "Such as?"

I rubbed my chin and looked him over. "I could turn you into a newt and send you scurrying under a rock. I could extinguish your belly fire permanently so you'd never have another hot meal. I could bind a storm cloud to you so it rained on you every time you left your cave. I could shrink you and keep you as a pet. I could—"

"All right! And what's to keep me from eating you now? I know I can't cook you while you're wearing that salve, but I don't mind raw food."

"You wouldn't eat a Dragon Friend, now would you?"

"You're not a … OH!" he said, squinting at me. If a dragon looks at a Dragon Friend in a special way, he can see a certain kind of aura. I'd been told that Dragon Friends were very rare, and that all dragons were honor-bound to treat them with respect. Of course that was in

133

the future, and I had no idea what they'd been treated like in the past.

"Why didn't you tell me straightaway?" said the dragon, looking disappointed. "Now I'll have to find something else for dinner, and I was so looking forward to eating you! I don't get to eat an intelligent meal very often."

"Would you feel better if I told you that I know of a wonderful place not too far from here where there are no humans?"

"Not really. I'm giving up the nomad life. Going to settle down right here. I've just decided—no more roaming for me."

"That's because of Millie's spell. You can give up roaming once you've reached the place I mentioned. Going to a new permanent home isn't really roaming, especially since it isn't far from here. You'll be able to see it once you get above the treetops."

"Where is it?"

"I'll tell you if you swear on your honor as a dragon that you won't ever go near humans again."

The dragon rolled his eyes and sighed. "On my honor as a dragon. Now where is this place?"

"In the Purple Mountains," I said, pointing in their general direction. "You can't miss them. And if you look in the center of the mountains, you'll find a natural arena with a pool of lava where you can have a good, long soak."

When I mentioned lava, the dragon's face brightened noticeably. "Lava, you say? That would feel good."

I nodded. "And the arena would be the perfect spot for the Dragon Olympics."

The dragon shook his head. "The Dragon Olympics have been held on an island for centuries. No one is going to want to move it now."

"It won't hurt to look, will it?"

"I suppose not. But if it isn't just as you say, I'll be back."

"Fair enough." As the dragon raised his wings to begin his first downbeat, I added, "Before you go, I didn't catch your name."

"It's Bone Cruncher. You may have heard of me. My motto is: *Flame once and ask questions later.*"

Nine

$\mathcal{I}$ used my farseeing ball to watch Bone Cruncher fly to the Purple Mountains. When he didn't come back, I turned myself into a bird again and flew to the castle, arriving shortly after dark. Everyone had been hard at work getting ready for the party. Men had carried hogsheads of ale from the cellar under the kitchen. Maids had removed the old rushes and debris from years past before scrubbing the floor of the Great Hall. The new rushes they'd spread were scented with herbs, making the room smell wonderful. Torches had been cleaned or replaced, tables and benches set around the room and colorful banners hung from the ceiling. Additional guests had arrived, bringing their servants with them.

Hazel had been busy using her own special talent. A table in the buttery was piled high with everlasting bouquets of roses, lilies and some dainty white flowers I didn't recognize, all looking as fresh as if they'd just been picked. I wondered if she'd really made enough or if I should make extra myself. I remembered Dyspepsia's words, and I had to keep myself from making too many changes. Flowering vines spread across the walls of the Great Hall, dripping pink and lavender blossoms. Sturdy trees had sprouted in the corners of the room, arching to meet the ceiling in cascades of delicate leaves and pale yellow blooms. Even the herbs sprinkled throughout the rushes on the floor looked as if they had taken root and were growing.

I found Millie talking to Jasper, Fenton and Eadric. Of the other young men who had volunteered to kill the dragon, one had changed his mind and gone home, while a second had disappeared downriver, chasing a water nymph. Eadric admitted that he and another knight had continued on until they realized that they were lost. After wandering around for most of the afternoon, they'd stumbled into a woodcutter who had showed them the way back to the castle.

Millie seemed relieved to see me and couldn't wait to talk to me alone. "I know Jasper needed help, but I felt awful leaving you the way I did," she said. "I worried about you all the way home. Did everything go well?"

I nodded. "That dragon shouldn't bother anyone around here again."

"When Garrid came back from hunting, I asked if he'd seen you. He said he hadn't and offered to go look."

"Did you tell him why I was in the woods?"

She shook her head. "I said you went for a walk and hadn't returned yet. I'd better go tell him that you're back. He was going to the kitchen first to drop off some rabbits he'd killed."

"I'll go," I said. "I'd like to meet this mysterious prince."

Finding Garrid wasn't hard this time. Since Millie had told me about him, I knew he had to be the tall, young blond knight I'd found chatting with the head cook. What Millie hadn't mentioned was that he was the handsomest prince in the castle—with his chiseled features and broad shoulders—and that he made all the other visiting princes, including Eadric, look like little boys.

Although everyone in the kitchen was working long hours to prepare for the party, they'd taken the time to inspect the rabbits he'd brought, already bled and gutted. While the cook praised the rabbits, giggling kitchen helpers fawned over Garrid, but I had the feeling he wasn't listening to any of them.

"Prince Garrid," I said as he left the kitchen. "May I have a moment of your time?"

He raised an eyebrow and said, "Do I know you?"

"I'm Emma. Millie said that you had offered to go looking for me, so I came to tell you that I'm back now."

A spark of recognition lit his eyes. "So you're Emma. I've heard all about you."

"You have?" I said, wondering what Millie might have told him.

Garrid patted me on the shoulder and smiled. The moment he touched me, I knew there was something different about him. Once I wouldn't have noticed it, but since my power had increased, I was sensitive to all the magic around me. In some way I didn't recognize, Garrid had magic. "Don't worry," he said. "Your secret's safe with me." Stepping around me, he strode off down the hall.

I felt cold all over, as if someone had opened a door on winter. My secret? Which secret was that? In this time and place I had too many to keep track of easily, too many things I didn't want people to know. What had Millie told him? That I was a witch? That I wasn't Frederika's daughter? Or had someone finally figured out that I didn't belong there at all?

I hurried back to the Great Hall to see Millie, but it was crowded when I arrived and everyone was talking excitedly.

"Did you hear?" said one of Queen Angelica's ladies to another. "Jasper and Fenton fought the dragon. Fenton says they chased it off."

"I heard he dealt it a grievous wound. The monster will probably bleed to death."

I wandered through the Hall, looking for Millie and hearing snatches of conversation.

"Fenton says it was enormous, the biggest dragon he'd ever seen."

"Its teeth were strong enough to cut through stone! He said it can chew up rocks and spit them out again."

"Have you seen Prince Jasper's armor? You can see where the dragon bit him."

I nodded. That much was true.

I finally found Millie, gnawing on her lip as she tried not to say a word. I knew how she felt, because I would have liked to squash a few rumors myself. I ground my teeth and tried to keep a pleasant expression on my face. "I'm going to bed now, Millie," I said. "I have to get up early tomorrow morning—very early."

Meeting Garrid had only made me more interested in him. Of all the princes courting Hazel, I had a feeling that he was the one I'd really have to watch. Apparently the only way to do that was to follow him when he went hunting. Maybe I could learn why he always went alone. Could he be using magic? When I tried to find Eadric to ask if he wanted to go with me, a squire told me that he was meeting with King Grunwald to discuss the best way to deal with werewolves and probably wouldn't be back until late. I waited in the Great Hall for another hour or so and was about to give up and go to bed when Eadric entered, talking to one of the squires.

Running to Eadric's side, I told the squire, "Excuse us. We have something important to discuss."

"Really?" said Eadric. "Like what?"

"That depends," I said after the squire had taken his leave. "What are you doing tomorrow morning?"

"Sleeping," Eadric said. "I haven't gotten much rest since I started sharing a room with five other princes."

"How would you like to go hunting with me?" I asked.

Eadric raised an eyebrow. "Hunting? You were never interested in hunting before. What do you plan to hunt?"

"Answers. I think it's about time someone followed Garrid and found out what he's really doing. Don't you think it's a little suspicious that he goes off by himself every day?"

"You think he's up to no good?" asked Eadric.

"I think he's up to something," I said. "He's too secretive to be innocent. Do you want to go with me? We'd have to leave early."

Eadric sighed. "Of course I'll go with you. I'll just have to sleep late another day. Maybe in a week or two."

It was easy to get up before dawn the next morning since I tossed and turned all night. When I couldn't lie in bed staring at the ceiling any longer, I dressed as quietly as I could so I wouldn't wake Millie. I met Eadric as we'd agreed, and we slipped downstairs to the Great Hall together. The guards were dozing at their posts, so we tiptoed past them to stand beneath one of the windows. With one eye on the closest guard, I turned Eadric and myself into bats, and we fluttered through the opening. Being able to see in the dark meant that we didn't need to wait until dawn when the guards would lower the drawbridge, and we could be ready and waiting when Garrid arrived. Besides, being a bat was fun when no one was chasing you.

We flew to the maze and called for Li'l, but it seemed to take forever before she answered. While I perched on her rosebush, Eadric darted back and forth, catching his breakfast of mosquitoes. "Where have you been?" I asked Li'l when she finally appeared.

"With Bugsy," she said, with a faraway look in her eyes.

Eadric gulped, swallowing a mosquito, and asked, "Who's Bugsy?"

Li'l sighed. "He's the most wonderful bat in the world. He doesn't know it yet, but I've decided to stay here with him."

"You mean until we go home?" I said.

"No, I mean forever. I love him, Emma. Bugsy is the perfect bat for me! I've never met anyone like him before, and I probably never will again. He's sweet and funny and thoughtful. I hope you'll be as happy with Eadric as I know I'm going to be with Bugsy!"

"Are you sure, Li'l?" I asked. This seemed totally bizarre, but maybe I had been too focused on the human world, or myself. "Have you really thought about this? If you stay here when Eadric and I leave, you'll be stuck in the past forever. And you don't know a thing about Bugsy! You don't even know his real name. You made up the name Bugsy, remember?"

"Past, future, what difference does it make to me, Emma? I'll miss you and Eadric, but my life is here with Bugsy. I know he's wonderful, and that's enough for me."

The sound of rattling chains and groaning wood announced the lowering of the drawbridge. It was happening earlier than was normal in my day, perhaps at Prince Garrid's request. A figure crossed the bridge and started down the road toward the forest, a bow slung over his shoulder.

I'm glad we came early, I thought and took to the air. "I'll talk to you about this later, Li'l. This is a very big decision." Li'l was my friend and I didn't want to leave her behind in the past, but I didn't see what I could do about it.

"Don't wake me if I'm asleep," said the little bat, yawning broadly.

It was generally unheard of for a member of my own royal family to go hunting without a group of friends or servants, and I was sure it was just as unusual in Millie's. Even so, Garrid strode alone down the road with great confidence, acting as if he was used to walking in the predawn dark by himself. Eadric and I flew behind him, staying far enough back that we could see him but where,

I hoped, he wouldn't see us.

The black of night was graying to morning when Garrid entered the woods, although it was still dark under the trees. If we hadn't been bats, we would have lost him altogether because he could move through the woods as silently as a shadow. We hung back, watching him when he stopped and cocked his head, then took off running so fast that we had a hard time keeping up. We lost him for a moment when he disappeared into a scrub-lined ravine. Something hit the ground with a crash, and a creature thrashed the foliage. I flew toward the sound and found Garrid bent over an injured doe, its limbs scrabbling feebly. Garrid's back was to me, but I could see the creature shudder, then grow still. After a time, Garrid straightened and stood up, lifting the deer as if it weighed nothing. Cradling the lifeless body in his arms, he climbed out of the gully and picked his way through the woods.

Eadric had joined me, and we were both following Garrid when he suddenly disappeared. It wasn't until we reached the spot where he'd vanished that we saw the opening to the cave. It was pitch black inside, and I expected him to light a candle or torch. He didn't, though, and we had to use our special sounds to find him.

Garrid was walking purposefully to a large hook set into the stone, moving as if he could see perfectly well.

After tying the deer's hind legs together with a strip of leather, he hung the carcass up to drain, setting a wooden bowl under it to catch the blood. Then, taking off his cape, he turned toward a large box set on a broad stone platform. I wondered what could be in the box that had to be kept so secret. Weapons perhaps? Something magical? Secret messages about an invasion? Yet of all the things I imagined, nothing could have surprised me more than what happened next.

He must have kept the hinges well oiled, for he lifted the lid without making a sound. I craned my neck to see when he reached inside, but all he did was take out a pillow and plump it between his hands. After setting the pillow back in the box, he climbed in, lay down and yawned. Although his two front teeth had looked normal when I spoke to him in the castle, they were now long, pointed and tipped with blood. I gasped when I realized what it meant. Handsome Prince Garrid, suitor to the future Green Witch of Greater Greensward and possibly my own ancestor, was a vampire!

Garrid must have heard me because he blinked and looked in our direction. He began to sit up, but we didn't wait to see what he'd do next. Beating our wings as fast as they could carry us, Eadric and I darted out of the cave and zipped between the trees. I didn't even try to talk to Eadric until the trees thinned and we could fly side by side.

"He's a vampire!" I said. "We'd better hurry back and tell Millie. I was sure he had some kind of secret, but I never thought it could be this bad." I didn't have anything against vampires as long as they kept to themselves, but I certainly didn't want Hazel to marry one. Not only did vampires exist on the blood of others, but they were known to carry all kinds of diseases, keep terrible hours and spend most of their time trying to convert everyone they met.

"I guess that explains where he goes every night," said Eadric. "And I thought he wasn't feeling well."

"He won't be," I said. "Not if he tries to marry into my family."

❧

We were out of the forest, speeding back to the castle, when we heard the nicker of horses and saw three men at the edge of a pond. We wouldn't have paid them any heed if we hadn't noticed that one was Fenton. He was arguing with two men I didn't know, a hulking man with a neck as big as his oversized biceps and a smaller man with a narrow face and pointed chin.

"Let's see what that's all about," I said to Eadric.

"I thought you were in a hurry to get back to the castle."

"I am, but Millie asked me to find out what I could about all the princes. We won't stay long."

We flew closer, hoping to hear their conversation. Circling the pond, we landed in the grass at the edge.

"I'm tired of your excuses!" said the shorter man. "You've owed me this money for a fortnight, and if I don't get it today, Georgie here will make you wish your ancestors had never been born." The big man grunted and narrowed his eyes until he looked fierce.

"I told you, you'll get it," said Fenton. "Once Princess Hazel chooses me, I'll push up the wedding date. Greensward's coffers have never been fuller. There's plenty there to pay off my debts and finance my return to the tournament circuit. I'm at the peak of my jousting career. The crowds love me, and so does the princess."

"What makes you think she'll choose you?"

"Because I'm her best choice, and she knows it. Some suitors have left already, scared off by the princess or that blasted dragon her father wanted us to kill. I'm the most attentive, as well as the best looking. She'll choose me; I'm sure of it."

"You'd better be right," said the smaller man. "Georgie doesn't like to be kept waiting."

As Prince Fenton mounted his horse and started back to the castle, we took to the air once again. I had a mission ahead of me. I had promised myself I would find out what I could about Millie's sister's suitors and I had plenty to tell, regardless of Dyspepsia's warning.

Ten

We reached the castle just as a small whirlwind landed at the foot of the drawbridge, depositing a plump, little witch with blue-tinged hair. It was only midday, yet some of the guests were already arriving. We landed in the garden and stayed there only long enough to become humans again before hurrying into the castle. I found Millie watching servants place tankards on tables set against the walls of the Great Hall.

"There you are, Emma," said Millie. "I've been looking for you all morning."

Someone opened a door leading into one of the corridors, and the scent of roasting meat wafted past us. Eadric sniffed the air like a hound and turned toward the kitchen. I almost expected to see him drool. "If you'll excuse me," he said, "I think a leg of mutton and a loaf of fresh bread are calling me. Do you need me now, Emma?"

I smiled and patted his arm. "Go ahead. I can tell her

by myself."

"Tell me what?" Millie asked as Eadric strode down the hall.

I led Millie away from the listening servants to a corner made private by the foliage of one of Hazel's trees. "I told you I had to get up early," I said. "I followed Garrid when he went hunting, and I learned his secret. Then I overheard Fenton talking, and I know what he's up to as well."

"I knew they were hiding things! What were they?"

I told her about Fenton first. She nodded and said she wasn't surprised. When I told her about Garrid, her eyes grew wide and she looked as horrified as I'd felt.

"A vampire here in our castle? We have to tell my father!" Millie gasped. "And Hazel! We have to tell her, too!"

"Shh!" I said. "Not so loud! We don't want to ruin the party."

"Ruin the party? I'm afraid she might ruin her life!" When Millie ducked under a branch and headed from the Hall, I hurried after her, concerned about what she might do.

Although we found Hazel right away, we weren't able to see her. She had locked herself in her room with her maids and seamstress and refused to let anyone else in.

"Hazel!" shouted Millie as she pounded on the door. "I need to talk to you!"

"Go away!" said her sister's muffled voice. "I'm busy! Ouch! Be careful, you wretch," she said to her seamstress. "You poke me with a needle again and I'll have you thrown into the moat."

"But Hazel," said Millie, "this is important! Open the door so I can talk to you."

"If it's that important, you can tell me from there," Hazel replied. "Otherwise go away!"

Since Millie didn't want to shout the news through the heavy wooden door, she decided to go looking for her father instead. Unfortunately, after searching the castle, we learned that King Grunwald had insisted that Eadric show him how to place escape-proof werewolf traps the way they did in Upper Montevista. No one knew exactly where Eadric and the king had gone.

We were still hoping to talk to Hazel and had gone back to wait outside her door when her mother saw us. Like most of the ladies of the castle, she had been primping since early morning and was already dressed for the party. Her gown of shimmering silver seemed to glow in the dimly lit corridor. "Ladies," she said, eyeing our everyday clothes, "I know you both have gowns more appropriate for tonight. Don't you think it's time you got ready?"

"Actually," said Millie, "we want to talk to Hazel first, but she won't let us in. Are you going to see her now?"

"I am, but you're not. You're to go to your chamber

immediately to change. Emma, see if you can do something with your hair. It looks like a bird has been nesting in it."

"But Mother," Millie wailed, "this is important! We learned something about Garrid that Hazel needs to know. If we can talk to her for just a minute—"

"You'll do no such thing, young lady. The last thing we need is for you to upset your sister. This is a very big day for her, and we don't need you ruining it. Now off to your room and that's an order!"

"We'll go, but would you please tell her for us? We found out that Garrid—"

"I said *now!*"

Millie ducked her head like an obedient daughter, but I could see the anger flash in her eyes. "Yes, Mother," she said, curtsying to the queen.

"Don't worry," I said as we hurried to her room. "We can tell Hazel at the party."

Millie nodded. "We'll think of something. I'm not giving up yet!"

We were near a window when something flew past, and I darted to the windowsill to look out. An old wizard seated on a battered door was spiraling down to land in front of the castle. As I watched, a half-dozen witches arrived on their brooms while several swooped in, seated on chairs laden with cushions. I stepped back when an enormous eagle with golden feathers stared at me through the window on his way to drop off the small, wizened woman he carried.

"Did you see all those witches?" I asked Millie, who had stopped beside me.

She nodded. "We'd better hurry and get dressed. I think the party is about to start. Your clothes are waiting for you. Mother sent them this afternoon."

I'd never been interested in fancy gowns, but for Millie's sake I tried to look excited. When we reached her chamber, I found a rust-colored tunic with a crimson surcoat lying on her bed.

"Tell me," said Millie as I wiped the last of the dragon salve off and slipped the tunic over my head. "After Hazel hears about Garrid, do you think she'll choose Jasper?"

"Probably," I said, glancing at Millie as soon as my head was free of the fabric. She looked distressed, making me wish I hadn't said anything.

When we were ready, Millie looked wonderful and far older than her thirteen years. Her hair was laced with a silver cord that glistened when she moved her head. Her tunic was the blue of a summer sky over which she wore a darker blue surcoat trimmed with silver. My clothes were plainer, but Millie had twisted my hair and looped it on top of my head in a way I thought was so flattering that I resolved to wear it that way when I got home. We were about to go out of the door when Millie took a delicate golden circlet out of a trunk by her bed. "I almost forgot Hazel's present," she said.

"Oh, no!" I said. "I was going to make one, but I've been so busy.... Give me a minute and let me think." I wanted to give her something she'd like, but I couldn't give her an obviously magical gift since I didn't want everyone to know that I was a witch. That didn't mean that I couldn't use magic to make it, however. If only I had something....

While Millie waited patiently by the door, I found the pouch I'd worn when I arrived and took out the candle stub. It was small, but it was enough. Only a few minutes later, Millie was in the Great Hall setting her golden circlet on the table set aside for gifts, leaving room for my wax replica of the castle, complete with miniature flowers.

It wasn't until we finally joined the party that I realized how difficult it might be to find Hazel. The Great Hall was crowded with guests of every shape and size. I saw hovering fairies no bigger than my thumb talking to hulking knights dressed in silk and leather. Other fairies were the size of the average human, but had a sparkle to their hair or a lilt in their voices that set them apart. Although none of the fairies was dressed like another, they all wore clothes derived from nature. Tunics of leaves or grass and gowns of flower petals or moonbeams clothed the dancers twirling across the floor to the melodies of human musicians.

The wizards were also dressed in fantastic clothes, having tried to outdo each other by using magic to make them. One wizard was dressed in a black robe that bore constantly changing numbers and symbols drawn in chalky white. Another wore a blue robe bedecked with floating clouds. A third, and the one that demanded the most attention, wore a mirrored robe and a tall, peaked hat that shot sparkling dust out of its pointed crown.

Although the wizards' clothes were interesting enough, it was the witches' clothes that made me catch my breath. I saw a gown that shimmered from one color to the next, encompassing the entire rainbow. A second was covered with splashing raindrops that seemed so real I almost expected to find water on the floor. My favorite, however, was a gown of moss green that smelled like the forest after a cleansing rain. It reminded me of my aunt Grassina and the kind of gowns she wore before the curse changed her.

There were normal people as well: relatives of Hazel's, inhabitants of the castle and the nobility from the surrounding area. Even though they were dressed in their finest clothes, they seemed drab and uninteresting when standing beside the magical guests.

"What color is Hazel wearing?" I asked Millie, craning my neck to search for her sister in the crowd.

"I don't know. She wouldn't tell me anything about it

except that it was much better than mine," Millie replied.

Human musicians played their instruments on a balcony above the Great Hall while dancers paraded below in the center of the room. Although most of the guests stayed at ground level, nearly half the fairy dancers cavorted in the air above them, creating a multihued spectacle with their fluttering wings. I stopped to watch the fairies for a moment, wondering if one of them would pronounce the curse that would do so much damage to my family.

A table had been set up at one end of the Hall. Laden with delicate, eggshell cups filled with dandelion wine and large, pewter tankards brimming with ale, it was the most crowded place in the room. A short distance away, another table stood covered with platters of hummingbird eggs, sugared violets and the herbed wings of some tiny bird. A third table supported platters of roasted pheasants and peacocks with reinserted feathers; suckling pigs glazed with honey, their mouths filled with sweet, red apples; and tureens of baked eels floating in a thick cream sauce. Eadric stood between a tall, thin man with jutting cheekbones and a handsome fairy dressed in hose and a tunic the color of new spring buds.

An already heaping plate in his hand, Eadric was reaching for one of the herbed wings when I stepped between him and the table, forcing him to look at me. "Emma," he said, "you look lovely."

"Thanks," I said, craning my neck to watch the people entering the room. "Have you seen Hazel?"

"Not since yesterday."

Millie squeezed between two heavyset witches and a long-haired warlock with a dragon emblazoned on the back of his robe. "Here, try this," Millie said, thrusting an eggshell cup into my hands.

The cup was so delicate that I was afraid to use it, but Millie and Eadric had no reservations. Common in the land of the fairies, the cups were sturdier than they looked. I followed their example and took a long sip, then started coughing when the sweet liquid burned my throat. This was no ordinary dandelion wine.

"The fairies brought the cups and the wine," Millie said, wiping her watering eyes.

"I believe it," I said, my voice a hoarse whisper.

Carrying our drinks with us, Eadric joined us in our search for Hazel. We were skirting the dancers in the middle of the room when I spotted Millie's mother approaching a group of witches in the far corner. A light breeze seemed to come from that part of the hall, stirring the banners hanging from the walls and the leaves of Hazel's trees.

Millie glanced at me. "You can tell that the witch Windifer is here. She can't go anywhere without her breezes. I forgot to warn you that some of Hazel's guests are a little unconventional."

"I didn't know there were so many witches in the area."

"They've come from all over," said Millie. "Hazel meets them at witches' gatherings. Let me introduce you to the ladies over there." Turning toward a cluster of witches, Millie led the way across the floor.

Four witches stood talking by the trunk of one of Hazel's trees. They all looked up when we approached, their eyes suspicious until they recognized Millie.

"Hello, princess," said a beautiful witch with hair and eyelashes of real gold and impossibly large, amber eyes. She wore a gown of brilliant red with tiny golden specks that gave off its own kind of heat. "It's a lovely party," she added in a deep, throaty voice.

Eadric's eyes seemed to glaze over when he saw her. I stumbled and stepped on his instep, which seemed to bring him back to the real world.

"I'm glad you're enjoying it," Millie said to the witch in red. Placing her hand on my back, she gave me a small nudge forward. "This is Emma, one of my cousins, and this," she said, "is her friend Eadric."

"How nice," said the golden-haired witch, dismissing us with a flick of her eyes.

I learned the names of all four witches, although I doubt they remembered mine. Scarletta, the witch dressed in red, was the only one who spoke to us.

I was trying to think of something polite to say when

the witches turned to stare past Millie at another witch who had come up behind her. Middle-aged, with dull, brown hair, everything about her was thin, from her thin face to her thin body to her thin, whiny voice. Unlike the other witches, she didn't look as if she had dressed for the occasion since she wore a faded, gray gown with a straggly, unraveling hem.

Scarletta sneered and said, "If it isn't Scrofula, looking as scrawny as ever. You'd best stay where you are or Windifer's breeze might blow you right out the door."

Scrofula's eyes narrowed. "Oh, I won't be the one to get blown away. We all know how full of hot air you are, Scarletta. It comes from puffing yourself up over your appearance every time you make yourself look twenty years younger, sister dear."

"Why," said Scarletta, "if we weren't guests in this castle, I'd—"

"You'd what?" said Scrofula, tilting her chin defiantly.

Millie whispered in my ear, "Emma, we have to do something. Those sisters are known to have the most awful fights."

Fights between witches often involved magic, putting everyone at risk. I shoved my cup at Scarletta and said, "Have you tried the dandelion wine?"

"What?" she asked, distracted for the moment.

"It's very good," I said. Taking a step toward her, I

did something I'd never done before; I pretended to trip. The dandelion wine sloshed out of the cup and down the front of Scarletta's gown, making the heated fabric sizzle.

"You clumsy girl!" said the witch, her voice suddenly shrill. "Why, I ought to—"

"Leave her alone, Scarletta," said her sister. "It's just a little wine. You aren't going to melt."

The golden-haired witch glared at Scrofula, then, with a crackle and a snap, Scarletta disappeared.

"How very rude!" said one of the other witches. Even I knew that it was impolite to vanish so abruptly at a social gathering.

"You were brilliant!" Millie told me as we continued our search for Hazel. "And pretending to be clumsy…."

"I've had a lot of practice with the real thing," I replied.

I was beginning to wonder if we'd ever find Hazel. Could she have decided to stay away from her own party? I was thinking of sending a page to look for her when a fairy I was passing fluttered her wings, slapping the side of my head with one.

"Oops," said the fairy, waving a nearly empty tankard of ale in my face. I backed away when the fairy burped, her ale-soaked breath strong even a few feet away. "This is good stuff!" she said, putting the tankard to her lips and draining it dry.

"The Swamp Fairy," said Millie.

I caught my breath with a gasp. Glancing at Eadric, I saw that his eyebrows were raised in surprise. We had met the Swamp Fairy once when we'd been frogs back in our own time. She'd been older then, yet when I looked at her more closely, I knew she hadn't changed much. Her blue hair didn't have the gray streaks it would have later on, and her flower-petal skirt looked fresher, but it was definitely the same fairy. Unlike witches, who are mortal, fairies live forever.

"Oh dear." The Swamp Fairy turned her empty mug upside down. "It's all gone. Better get more!" she said in a cheery voice. Fluttering her wings, she rose straight into the air, nearly colliding with a dancing couple. "Watch where you're going!" she declared.

We circled the room, studying the mingling guests, when a bell chimed, light and sweet. "Attention, every-one!" called a voice as the volume in the room dwindled.

"There she is," Eadric said, gesturing toward the raised dais. Flanked by her mother's ladies-in-waiting, Hazel stood facing the dance floor. Her clothes were magnificent; both her tunic and her surcoat had been made from cloth of gold, and diamonds sparkled in her hair.

"I have to get up there," Millie whispered as she looked for a way to reach her sister. Seeing an opening between two knights, she squeezed past them while I followed close on her heels.

"Thank you for coming," said Hazel. She was so loud it sounded as if her voice was magically amplified. "I'm happy to celebrate my birthday with all my closest friends."

"Who is that?" asked a fairy with spiky green hair, pointing at Hazel.

"Shh!" hissed the people around him. I saw another gap between two groups of witches and hurried to get through.

"I'm about to open my presents," Hazel said. "And I'd like to thank you all now."

"She does that so she doesn't have to thank anyone afterward," whispered Millie.

It took some time for Hazel to open all the gifts because there were so many, but it gave me the opportunity to work my way closer to the dais. The presents from her relatives were fairly boring—clothes mostly and a few pieces of jewelry. The princes had given her cups embedded with gems, bolts of rare fabrics and boxes with lids of hammered gold. The witches gave her gifts such as a farseeing ball, a ring for carrying secret potions and a new broom. The membership in the Apple of the Month Society—one plain and one poisoned apple per month—was more original, although it earned the gift giver scowls from the people around her.

When Hazel unwrapped a hand mirror, she held it up

so everyone could see it, then asked the traditional question, "Mirror, mirror in my hand. Who's the fairest in the land?"

A light shimmered over the mirror's surface. "Not you, missy," it said. "You cheat at dice!"

Blushing, Hazel handed the mirror to one of her mother's ladies-in-waiting. "This mirror doesn't work right. Put it with the others we need to get fixed."

We had almost reached Hazel when she began to open the presents from the fairies. Suddenly even the most bored guests were taking an interest. Everyone had already seen the cups and the dandelion wine, but the silver flute that played itself and asked for requests after each selection was new. So was the pink flower-petal skirt that came with directions. "Water twice a week," read Hazel from the attached leaf.

There were other musical gifts and a few that were meant to make the wearer more beautiful, like the crown that made her glow with a golden light. A tiny gilded cage held a hummingbird that laid golden eggs. "Stingy," said a lavender-haired fairy near me when the fairy who'd given the gift beamed smugly. "She could have given the princess a bigger bird."

Another gift, and the most exciting one as far as I was concerned, was from an elderly fairy dressed in willow leaves. Everyone waited quietly as she climbed onto the dais. When she reached Hazel's side, she showed her a ring, the very same ring I would wear many years later on my finger, and spoke in a loud, clear voice that carried throughout the hall. "My gift to you, sweet Princess Hazel, will last for all generations. From this day on, the nicest and most powerful witch in your kingdom will be the Green Witch. With this gift comes greater power as well as greater responsibility, for the Green Witch must be the kingdom's protector, using her magic to ensure the safety of its inhabitants, whether human- or fairy-kind." Taking the princess's hand in hers, the fairy slipped the ring on Hazel's finger and said, "I name you the first Green Witch."

A ripple of applause ran through the room. Smiling, Hazel curtsied to the fairy and thanked her. As the elderly fairy climbed down from the dais, I watched the first Green Witch turn her hand this way and that to admire the ring on her finger.

"Look at her," whispered Millie. "She likes the ring, but I doubt she paid any attention to the part about taking care of the kingdom."

"Now it's my turn," called out the green-haired fairy who hadn't known Hazel. "I didn't know what to bring you—" he said, striding toward the dais.

"Since he crashed the party and didn't know anyone here," said a fairy no taller than my knee whom I hadn't noticed, even though he was standing beside me. His broad red cap dotted with white spots made him look like a mushroom, and he had an earthy kind of smell.

"—so I decided to wait for inspiration before choosing a gift," continued the green-haired fairy. "That last gift inspired me!" Flourishing his hand in the air, he presented Hazel with a tapestry that seemed to appear out of nowhere.

"What is he, a wizard or a fairy?" asked the mushroom.

Hazel glanced at the tapestry and frowned. "Let us see," called someone from the back, so she turned it around and held it up.

It was one of the tapestries that hung in my tower room and showed the Green Witch from behind as she watched a retreating enemy from the battlements. Only now the Green Witch had long blond hair instead of auburn like mine.

"What is it?" someone shouted.

The fairy's grin slipped when he saw the puzzled expressions. "It's the Green Witch defending the castle, of course," he said, pointing at the picture. "It will always show the current Green Witch, no matter who she is."

"It's very nice, I'm sure," said Hazel, but it was clear that she was disappointed. When the deflated-looking fairy had rejoined the other guests, the princess smiled again. "And now for the announcement that you've all been waiting to hear."

"Oh, no!" said Millie. "I'm too late!"

"Wait!" shouted a voice, and Prince Jasper pushed his way to the front. "Before you tell us who you plan to marry, I have something to say that I'd hoped to say in private."

You too? I thought.

"I owe it to you to be honest," said the prince. "I am not worthy of you. I have fallen in love with another and can never give you the love that you deserve."

"Forget it," Hazel said, brushing him off with a wave of her hand. "I wasn't going to choose you anyway."

"You weren't?" Millie squeaked.

"I'm going to marry Prince Garrid! We've made our plans. We'll be married within the month."

"You can't marry him!" Millie said, pushing past the little mushroom fairy. "Garrid is a vampire!"

Hazel glanced at her and shrugged. "So?" she said. "Nobody's perfect!"

The crowd had begun to get restless when they realized that Hazel had received her last present. Hazel must have noticed this, because she held up her hand and called out, "One last thing! Make sure you see me before you go. I have gifts for each of you!"

Even the dour-faced witches looked happy after hearing this. Since she hadn't let me help, I'd just have to hope that she had enough for everyone.

Eleven

The party went on until dawn, but by the time the faint light of a rainy day had crept through the windows high on the wall of the Great Hall, nearly all of the guests had gone home. The normal, human guests—including the relatives and the unsuccessful suitors—had already gone to bed, even though they wouldn't leave until the next day. After staying up with us all night, Eadric had wandered off to the kitchen in search of breakfast. Only Hazel, Millie and I were still in the Great Hall waiting to say farewell to the last of the guests.

A trestle table had been set up to hold the everlasting bouquets. When the final guest came to claim her present, I was delighted to note that there were still two bouquets left, even though some guests had taken more than their share. It looked as though Hazel had enough bouquets for everyone.

"You're sure she's the last one?" I said, gesturing toward the table where Scrofula was chatting with Hazel.

"I'm positive," said Millie. "We had the pages look everywhere, just as you suggested. They found her in the garden and brought her here to get her gift."

"Good," I said. "Then maybe it really is over."

When Millie and I went to the table to say good-bye to Scrofula, she was reaching for a second bouquet. "My sister left early. I'll give it to her the next time I see her."

"So we still had enough," I said, watching Scrofula leave.

"I don't know why you're so worried," said Millie. "If we'd run out, Hazel could have made more."

"Made more what?" asked Garrid.

I hadn't noticed him come into the room, and apparently neither had Hazel. "Where have you been?" she asked, her gaze frosty. "I've been looking everywhere for you."

"I had things to take care of so I could concentrate on you this morning," he said, putting his arms around her. "We still have a lot to talk about."

I turned away when they started to kiss, and that's when I noticed something small and black fly in through a window and land in one of Hazel's trees. I slipped away to investigate. "Li'l, is that you?" I whispered.

A little head popped up from behind a branch. "Why didn't you tell me there were trees in this castle?" Li'l asked. "I could have stayed in one of these."

"They weren't here before," I said. "Hazel grew them

for the party. I'm glad you came. I was just about to go look for you. I'll be leaving as soon as I say good-bye to Millie and Hazel. The party is over. Most of the guests have left. Since there were enough gifts for everyone, no one cast a curse."

Li'l crawled around the branch until she was hanging upside down. "I didn't come to say good-bye now. I was looking for Bugsy. He was late coming to see me, and then he acted funny. I was worried about him, so I followed him after he took me home. He came to the castle. He has to be around here somewhere."

"I haven't noticed any other bats, but then I haven't been looking. Maybe I should go—"

Someone groaned on the other side of the tree, loudly enough that even Millie heard it. "Emma, was that you?" she asked from halfway across the Hall.

"No," I whispered, tiptoeing around the trunk. "It was…."

The Swamp Fairy sat up and looked at me, rubbing her eyes with her knuckles. "What day is it?" she asked.

"The day after my birthday party," said Hazel, joining us by the tree. "Everyone else has gone home. I thought you'd left already."

Li'l pulled her wings closer to her sides, trying to make herself look smaller and less conspicuous. "Is that a bat?" asked Hazel, backing away from the tree. "What is a bat doing in my castle?" She looked around frantically, spotting a dirty tankard on a table. "Get out of here!" she hollered, snatching up the tankard and hurling it at Li'l.

The tankard missed Li'l by inches, but was close enough to frighten her. Releasing her hold on the trunk, she fell a few feet, then began flapping frantically. Hazel reached for another tankard and was about to throw it, when Garrid leapt in front of her and shouted, "No! Don't hurt her. That's Li'l!"

Frightened, Li'l blundered onto the table where the ale had been served. "Oh my, oh my!" she cried, knocking over an empty eggshell cup and dragging her wing in a puddle of spilled ale.

I ran over to the table to help her, but Garrid was there first. He caught her in his hands, then cupped her gently and said, "Don't be afraid, Li'l. It's me, Bugsy!"

"What do you mean, *Bugsy*?" demanded Hazel, her face turning a deep red. "Why are you acting like you know that bat? What's going on, Garrid?"

Garrid looked up. "Hazel, I—"

With Garrid distracted, it was easy for Li'l to wriggle free. She slipped out of his hands and darted toward the window.

"Li'l! No!" Garrid called after her.

"Pardon me," said the Swamp Fairy, massaging her temples with her fingertips. "If you'll just give me my guest gift, I'll be on my way."

"Li'l!" shouted Garrid, more loudly than before. A shadow passed over him, there was a puff of cool, dank air and Garrid turned into a bat. Hazel shrieked when he followed Li'l out the window.

"Now do you believe me?" Millie asked. "Vampires do that kind of thing."

"About that gift—" the Swamp Fairy began.

Red faced, Hazel turned on the fairy. "Stop pestering me!" she screamed. "Can't you see that I'm in the midst of a crisis! I don't have any more of those bouquets, anyway, so just go away and leave me alone!"

I bit my lip as the Swamp Fairy's eyes grew hard and her tired face turned angry. "I can't believe you said that to me!" she said to Hazel. "No one talks to the Swamp Fairy like that and gets away with it!" The air around the fairy began to shimmer. Raising her arms to the ceiling, the fairy called out in a loud voice,

> For being rude to fairy-kind,
> There is a price to pay, you'll find.
> From those who could not be polite,
> We do not soon forget a slight.

> If, after your fifteenth year,
> You should touch a flower, dear,
> All your prettiness shall fade
> Leaving you an ugly maid.

Your beauty gone, your sweetness, too,
No one will want to be with you.
A nasty spirit, ugly face,
You won't be welcome anyplace.

Daughters of your family, too,
Will become nasty just like you.
If after the fated hour,
They should touch a single flower.

This curse shall last until the day
A true love's kiss can help convey
That he looks past her nasty ways
To see her true self in her gaze.

Thunder boomed and green lightning flashed through the window as the fairy left the Hall. When Millie cried out, Hazel turned on her and said, "Don't be stupid! I'm a witch! My magic is more powerful than anything a fairy can throw at me."

I staggered, shocked by what had just happened. I'd come to their time to hear the curse, but had begun to hope that the fairy might not pronounce it after all. Although I'd worried about changing history, I'd meddled where I probably shouldn't have. It didn't seem to have had any real effect, however, since the curse had been cast anyway, making me feel like a failure even though I'd done what I'd originally set out to do.

Millie and Hazel were arguing when I went outside to find Li'l and Garrid. *Li'l's heart must be broken,* I thought, dashing past the guards and into the garden. It was pouring rain, and I stepped in a puddle the moment I left the drawbridge, soaking my shoes and the hem of my gown.

I found the two bats in the spot where I usually met Li'l. Perched on a rosebush beside Garrid, she was so agitated that she couldn't sit still. "You were one of the princess's suitors, weren't you?" she asked Garrid. "What did you plan to do? Were you going to marry her and never tell me? It's not going to work."

"I'm sorry, Li'l," he said. "I didn't mean for this to happen. I never wanted to hurt you. I think you're wonderful. I'd choose you if I could, but I'd already offered my hand to Hazel. If only you and I had met sooner."

"Well, we didn't, and now you're going to marry *her.* And to think I wanted to stay here with you after Emma went home. Emma," she said, turning to face me. "When are you leaving?"

"As soon as I change my clothes and say good-bye. I heard the curse, so I know what needs to be done."

"Then I'm going to the castle with you. The sooner we get back where we belong, the happier I'll be!"

I sneaked Li'l into the castle inside my sleeve, which was just as well since the rooms were bustling with people clearing off the tables and hauling away the trash.

After I'd changed back into my own clothes, I gathered my pouch and farseeing ball and went downstairs to the Great Hall to say good-bye. We heard the sound of wailing before we reached the door. Millie was gone, but Queen Angelica and her ladies-in-waiting were there, tears streaming down their faces.

"This is terrible," the queen wailed. "You've offended a fairy! We've tried so hard to get along with the fairies, and now this!"

Hazel rolled her eyes. "Don't be ridiculous, Mother. It doesn't mean a thing. I'm a witch. Fairies can't cast curses on witches!"

"Is that true?" Li'l whispered.

"No," I whispered back.

"Look. I'll prove it to you," Hazel said, "and you'll see that you're being silly."

"Don't!" screamed her mother as the princess reached for an enormous blossom dangling from a vine on the wall. There was an audible gasp in the room when Hazel buried her face in the flower.

"Princess Hazel," said Garrid, standing by the door, a man once again. His eyes were sad, and he looked more dejected than a hound left behind from the hunt. "I must apologize for what just happened. I will marry you, if you'll still have me."

"Of course I'll have you," said Hazel, taking her face out of the flower. But she had changed already, and the difference was shocking. No longer lovely, her eyes were small and beady, her nose and chin so long and pointed that they nearly met in front of her mouth. Bumpy warts had sprouted on her cheek, and her once-lustrous hair was thin and straggly.

After one glance at her elder daughter, the queen shrieked and fled the room while two of her ladies-in-waiting fainted. Garrid's face turned ashen, but he stood his ground without flinching.

"But you're going to have to change your ways, bat boy," said Hazel. "No going out at night with your friends. No more all-day hunting trips. You'll stay home with me and do what I tell you. Your taste in clothes is pitiful, so I'll pick out what you'll wear. Starting tomorrow, you'll…."

Garrid looked horrified. With each new pronouncement, he stepped backward, away from his future bride. She was still listing the changes she would make in his life when he reached the doorway.

"I know you have an eye for the ladies, so I can't trust you. I'll need to know where you are every minute of the day. You'll report to me and—"

"Never!" shouted Garrid before he turned and bolted out the door.

"You're not getting away that easily, mister!" shrieked Hazel. She had a gleam in her eye when she passed me at a run. Even after they left the room, I could hear their feet pounding the stone floor. When I felt a cool, dank puff of air, I knew that Garrid had turned back into a bat.

"Well," said Li'l. "I guess he changed his mind. But I haven't changed mine. Emma, can we go home now?"

Twelve

The castle was in an uproar after Hazel disappeared, and Eadric, Li'l and I couldn't wait to go home. Relatives afraid of the curse were throwing their belongings into wagons and onto the backs of packhorses as they rushed to leave early. Prince Fenton was already gone, having taken one of the ladies-in-waiting with him. The queen had retreated to her chamber along with the rest of her ladies. No one went near King Grunwald, who was bellowing that he'd find the fairy and force her at sword point to change his daughter back.

Eadric wanted to leave right away, but I insisted that we find Millie before we go. We finally located her in a quiet antechamber, far from the chaos in the rest of the castle. She was talking to Jasper, and I could tell from her expression that something wonderful had happened. Jasper was holding both of her hands, and he didn't look as if he planned to let go.

"Emma, I want you to be the first to hear the news," Millie said. "Jasper told me that I'm the one he loves. He wants to ask my father for my hand in marriage."

"And what did you say?" I asked her, although I was sure I already knew the answer.

"I told him yes," she said, blushing, "as long as he can get Father's permission. We won't actually get married for a few more years, though. Hazel was waiting until she turned sixteen to choose a suitor, and I'm sure Father will expect me to wait as well."

"Did you tell him about … you know?" I asked.

"If you mean my magic, yes, I told him that I'm a witch," said Millie.

"She told me," said Jasper. "It doesn't make a difference one way or the other. I'd want to marry her no matter what. I'm just glad she's willing to marry someone as ordinary as me."

"I know what you mean. That's how I feel about Emma," said Eadric, giving me a quick kiss on the cheek.

"I see you already have the ring," I said to Millie, pointing at her hand.

Millie looked down and saw the green ring on her finger. "How did that get there?"

"That ring belongs to the Green Witch," I said. Millie opened her mouth to protest, until I held up my hand. "No, I don't think you took it from Hazel. She's no longer the Green Witch. You are."

"How is that possible?" Millie asked. "She received the title yesterday."

"Think about what the fairy who gave it to her said. The nicest and most powerful witch in Greater Greensward will be the Green Witch. I never thought Hazel was very nice, but that fairy must have thought so and the ring must have been waiting to see for sure. Anyway, Hazel didn't believe in the fairy's curse, so she touched a flower to prove she was right. The curse took effect, turning Hazel nasty—certainly nastier than she used to be. That means that you're the nicest, so...."

"I'm the Green Witch? But you're much more powerful than I am, so why didn't you get the title? And what about those other witches at the party? Surely they were more qualified, too."

"The Green Witch has to be from Greater Greensward, so that eliminates a lot of witches. I already am the Green Witch, back where I came from. There can be only one at a time, and this is not my time."

Millie's hand flew to her mouth. "I think I understand now. You aren't really my cousin, are you?"

"No," I said, "but we are related." If Millie was the first real Green Witch, she and Jasper were probably my ancestors. Somehow, I found that thought very comforting.

"I'm never going to see you again, am I?" Millie

asked, her eyes welling up with tears.

"No, I'm afraid not. But in a way, you'll always be with me."

"I guess so," she said, glancing at Jasper. He raised one eyebrow, but she just patted his arm reassuringly and turned to Eadric. "It was nice meeting you, Eadric. Take good care of Emma."

"I always do," he said. I don't think he understood why Millie and I grinned at each other.

Since I hate long good-byes, we left as quickly as we could. I knew how to end the curse, although it wasn't going to be easy, and I was anxious to get home and try it.

❧

The oubliette was empty when we got there, which meant that we didn't have to disguise ourselves. Since we knew what to expect, Eadric held on to Li'l with one hand and put his arms around me while I released a little of the dragon's breath from the bottle.

I needed to come up with an event to mark the time of our return, but all I could think of was the tournament that my father had planned to start the day before my birthday.

> I need to go to the future now,
> To the time from which I came,

Before the day of the tournament
And the start of the very first game.

We were in the dark tunnel almost instantly. The wind tumbled us around like drunken jesters. *This won't last forever,* I promised myself, as the air began to grow thicker. When the roar died down enough so that I could hear Li'l moan, I noticed that the air smelled sour again. Then the high-pitched whine started, and something shoved us through the cloying layer.

This time we hit the floor rolling and didn't stop until we bumped into something solid. Hard objects rained on my head as I tried to get my bearings.

"Help!"

"Watch out!"

"Oh, nooooooo!"

When something landed on my back and bit me, I knew right away what had happened. I'd bumped into the pile of skulls, dislodging the top layer. I rolled over, trying to get away from the skulls, and ended up on my side.

"Mmph," said Li'l in a muffled voice. "Get off me!"

"Sorry!" I said, struggling to sit up. I opened my eyes and closed them again right away. The room was bright, or seemed that way to eyes grown used to the tunnel. I saw the reason when I opened them to little slits, glanced toward the ceiling and saw the witches' light I'd left behind.

While Li'l shook the dust from her wings, I looked around the oubliette. Grandfather was gone and the pile of skulls was in disarray, but otherwise it looked much the same as it had when we left.

"Wouldn't you know it," said one of the skulls that I'd knocked to the floor. "It's that clumsy girl and her suitor again."

"Don't be rude," said a skull still on the pile. A hand raised up from the mound of bones and waggled its fingers at me. "Hello," said the skull. "Nice to see you again. Did you have a nice trip?"

"Very funny," said the first skull. "And you said *I* was rude."

"It was fine, thank you," I said, picking up a skull and setting it back on the pile.

"Here, Emma," said Eadric. "I'll do that." Ignoring the grumbling from the skulls, Eadric restacked the pile, making it neater than it had been before.

As Eadric set the last skull on the pile, I reached into my purse and said, "I have Hubert's medallion. Thanks for letting me use it."

"Hubert, come get your medallion," shouted one of the skulls.

The pile of bones shuddered while a hand rose up and twiddled its fingers. I handed it the medallion. The fingers fumbled until they had a good grip, then the hand sank back into the heap.

"Can we go yet?" asked Li'l.

"Before you go," said one of the skulls, "we wondered if you could leave that ball of light here. It's nice having light in the old place, even if there isn't much to see."

"All right," I said. "If you really want it."

"What about us?" said Eadric. "How are we supposed to see in the dark?"

"Don't worry," I said. "I know what I'm doing."

I said the spell that changed Eadric and me into bats.

"Very nice!" said a skull, and a scattering of hands in the bone pile turned to each other and applauded.

"Bats again?" said Eadric. "Couldn't we try something else?"

"Not if we're flying in the dark," I said, testing my wings.

When we flew out of the oubliette, we found that the dungeon had changed again. The magic loose in the dungeon was always rearranging the walls. A new wall blocked the passage we'd used before, so we had to take a different way that twisted and turned in all sorts of strange angles. We ran into magic fog only once, and that was such a small patch that I had scarcely noticed it before we were out of it again.

We were passing through the guardroom when we came upon a trio of ghosts. "How do you plan to scare people tonight?" asked a hollow-voiced specter. "I'll wait until they sit down to supper, then scream whenever someone sticks his knife in his meat."

"I'll haunt the bedchambers," said another. "A bloody ax at midnight always gets a good reaction."

A ghost with a purplish tinge to his aura spoke next. "I can top both of you. I'm going to dress like a guard and haunt the privy. I'll hide in the hole and when anyone sits down I'll wail, 'Who goes there? State your business!'"

The other ghosts snickered, but I was too angry to think anything was funny. Most of the castle ghosts were friendly; the few who weren't stayed in the dungeon and never bothered anyone upstairs. Yet these ghosts were plotting to terrorize the castle's inhabitants, and I didn't think this would be their first night to do so. I was sure that they couldn't have changed so much unless someone had influenced them, and I had a good idea who that someone might be.

When we finally reached Grassina's room, I turned us back into humans before I knocked on the door. I had a lot to say to Grassina, and it would have a bigger impact if I didn't say it as a bat. No one answered when I knocked, so I opened the door and peeked inside, hoping to find her anyway. Grassina wasn't there, but Blister the rat was sitting on her moldy blanket, gnawing an old melon rind.

"You're back," he said, twitching his pointy, little

nose at me. "Too bad you made it. If you're looking for Grassina, she isn't here."

"Where is she?" I asked.

The rat smirked. "How would I know? I'm stuck down here all day, although I have been thinking about taking a trip upstairs."

"Go right ahead," I said. "And I'll have the biggest, meanest cat that you've ever seen waiting for you."

Blister snarled, baring his teeth. "Maybe I'll wait."

Eadric and Li'l had been poking around on Grassina's workbench, examining water-filled jars containing a baby octopus, a baby shark and a tiny crab. A small cage held a tiny hamster covered with long, flowing fur.

"What's this?" Eadric asked, lifting the lid off my aunt's cauldron. "It smells like rotting cabbage."

Snatching the lid from his hand, I said, "Don't touch anything! You never know what she's cooking up." I sneaked a peek into the cauldron, where a lavender substance bubbled and seethed.

"Put that down," squealed Blister. The mangy rat scurried across the floor and up the leg of Grassina's workbench. "Ooh, Grassina's going to be so mad! No one's supposed to touch that except her!" He chattered his teeth and tried to knock the lid from my hand.

"Watch out!" I said, stepping back a pace.

Blister rose up on his hind legs and reached for the lid.

A large bubble popped, splattering glowing droplets, and a few landed on the agitated rat. Blister squealed and fell onto the table, rolling back and forth as if his fur was on fire. When he started to shrink, I thought my eyes were tricking me; but when his fur began to grow, I was sure it was because of Grassina's concoction. His once-patchy fur became long and luxurious. No longer a muddy brown, it was a deep, velvety color. Even as I watched, his fur grew until it was so long that his face and limbs were hidden in a thick, brown mat. "I told you not to touch it!" he whined, his voice muffled by fur. "You stupid nitwits are always prying into other people's business. A gnat has more brains than you three put together!"

Another bubble rose to the top, and I clapped the lid on before it could pop. Some lavender dust had been left on the rim of the cauldron, but the lid dislodged it and it drifted down, settling on the ranting rat, coating him with a thin layer. "You're morons," the rat continued. "You must be the stupidest, clumsiest creatures I've ever seen. If I was half as clumsy as you, I'd—"

"That's enough out of you," I said. "If you can't say anything nice, don't say anything at all!" It was something I'd heard the cook tell gossiping scullery maids and it had always made them stop. Even so, I was surprised when Blister's mouth closed with a snap.

Li'l blinked and glanced up at me. "Do you suppose the dust did that, too?"

"Maybe," I said. "Too bad we didn't find it sooner."

I thought about leaving a note for my aunt saying that I wanted to talk to her, then decided that she probably wouldn't read it. When we went upstairs, Li'l flew to the tower to take a nap while Eadric left to check on Bright Country and I went to talk to Grassina about the ghosts.

I stopped to ask a maid if she'd seen my aunt. The girl had a strange, panicky look in her eyes, although I didn't think much of it until she spoke. Her mouth opened and her lips moved, yet nothing came out except a shiny bubble that grew bigger the longer she talked. When she closed her mouth, the bubble floated free and drifted up to the ceiling.

I tried to say, *What's wrong with you?* but I couldn't make any sort of sound no matter how hard I tried. Instead I felt a bubble form between my own lips. The more I tried to talk, the bigger the bubble grew. I gestured, trying to tell the maid that I didn't understand what was happening, but I couldn't make her understand *me.* The maid shrugged and pointed at the ceiling. I looked up, and my jaw dropped. The ceiling was covered with hundreds of shiny bubbles.

Grassina, I thought, grinding my teeth.

I went to the Great Hall, determined to find my aunt, but I found my mother instead. When she saw me, she handed me a long pin and held up one of her own. I was confused. "Mother," I said, "what's going on?" or at least that's what I tried to say. A large bubble floated from my lips, but before it had gone far, my mother stabbed it with her pin. The bubble popped and my words came out as clearly as I had intended.

Then it was my mother's turn. She pointed at my pin and opened her mouth, letting loose one bubble after another. Although I tried to pop them and listen to what they said, Mother was talking so fast that it came out in a crazy jumble.

"Eadric's parents will arrive this afternoon," said one bubble.

"You'll wear them whether you like them or not," said another.

"This is all Grassina's fault."

"Where have you been?"

"I've had three gowns made for you."

"The tournament starts tomorrow."

"We had to order additional tents."

"You never sat for your fittings."

"I can't get anything done."

"She's driving us mad."

Although I probably missed more bubbles than I popped, I did learn that Eadric's parents would be arriving that afternoon and that the spell had brought me back the day prior to the beginning of the tournament, which meant that I didn't have much time. Before I did anything else, I had to locate Grassina and make her do something about the bubble spell.

I searched the castle, questioning everyone I met, but no one had seen my aunt. It took longer than it should have since everyone spoke in bubbles. When no one inside the castle seemed to be able to tell me where she might be, I decided to look outside the castle walls and finally found my aunt kneeling at the edge of the moat trying to coax a slime monster out of the water. The monster, a large transparent sac filled with dozens of eyes floating in pale green goo, left a slimy sheen on anything it touched. It moved by pulling its boneless body on dripping, shapeless feelers.

"What's this all about, Grassina?" I said, surprised that words came out of my mouth and that I was no longer making bubbles. "You confined the voice-bubble spell to the upper floors of the castle, didn't you? It doesn't work outside the walls or in the dungeon."

Grassina patted the slime monster, then wiped her hand on her gown. "Good for you, lady genius. How long did it take you to figure out that one?"

Gurgling softly, the slime monster slipped back into the moat.

"We're having company soon," I said, "and we can't have your voice-bubble spell working when they get here."

Grassina made a face at me that would have been

frightening if I hadn't known her. "Why not?" she asked. "I like bubbles. Don't you?"

"Of course I like bubbles, but I think you like them too much. And if that's the case...." The spell was simple and I'd said half of it before she even figured out that it was a spell.

Since you like the bubbles so,
In a bubble you must go.
In that bubble you will stay
Till your bubbles go away.

Sound can't pass from inside out
Even if you scream or shout.
If you want to be set free,
End your own spell, that's the key.

Grassina threw up her hand to ward off the spell, but it was too late. A giant, shimmering bubble formed around my aunt, who let out an anguished wail that was cut off when the bubble was complete. Although I couldn't hear her, I could see her quite clearly and I could tell that she was furious. Her face contorted with anger, she pounded on the bubble with her fists. Nothing happened until, very slowly, the bubble began to roll in the direction she was pounding. I could tell she was shouting at me, but I still couldn't hear anything she said.

The bubble fell into the water with a splash that drenched my gown and swept the slime monster halfway across the moat. Grassina thrust her hands against the side when the bubble wobbled and bounced. She tried to keep her balance as it floated across the water, but something big must have rammed the bubble from below, because it suddenly shot into the air, then slammed back farther down the moat. Grassina fell to her knees, and I could see her staring into the water. Her lips were moving when the monster surfaced. A cross between a fish and some sort of lizard, it had long, sharp teeth, jagged fins and a serrated tail. Whatever spell she'd said didn't seem to have any effect, but neither did the monster's teeth when it tried to bite the bubble. While I couldn't hear Grassina, the screech of the monster's teeth scraping the bubble made me cringe.

The bubble continued to float, nudged by the monster's butting snout. Grassina's face turned red, and little veins stood out in her forehead. She glared at me until the monster hit the bubble again, knocking it across the water. Apparently the monster had made her angry enough that revenge had become more important than her bubbles. After glancing at me one last time, she nodded and recited a spell. When she'd finished, the bubble shimmered more brightly than before, then burst with a loud POP.

Grassina screamed as she fell into the water, but the

sound from the castle was even louder. All the words that had been trapped in bubbles since the moment she had cast the spell were suddenly let loose. I was delighted until I noticed that my aunt had disappeared beneath the surface and had yet to come up. Although I knew she could swim, only Grassina knew what kinds of monsters she'd let loose in the moat. I was trying to decide what I could do to help her when her head broke the surface and she gasped for breath.

"Do you need a hand?" I asked.

She shook her head and turned around just as the monster rose up out of the water and eyed her hungrily. It was huge, nearly as long as the moat was wide, and it certainly frightened me. I heard Grassina mutter something, although I couldn't hear what she said, but then I wasn't really paying attention because the monster had started to move. Sweeping its tail from side to side, it bore down on my aunt, who was still bobbing in the water. Before I could warn her, she disappeared with a bright yellow flash, and the biggest shark I'd ever seen was swimming in her place. The monster swerved and turned tail, speeding away from my aunt. Snapping her jaws, Grassina took off after it, diving below the surface as they disappeared around the curve in the moat. And to think I'd been worried about her!

Thirteen

I found Eadric in the stable brushing Bright Country. "Your parents are supposed to arrive this afternoon," I told him. "I need to go now if I'm to be back before then."

"What do you intend to do?" he asked.

"Go see the Swamp Fairy, of course. I'll ask her to remove the curse. It was laid so long ago, I can't imagine that she'd still hold a grudge against our family. She's probably forgotten all about it."

Eadric nodded. "Just give me a minute to get ready."

"There's no need—"

He sighed and rubbed his forehead as if it ached. "We've been through this before. I don't want you going alone if there's even the chance that it might be dangerous. I'm going with you and that's all there is to it. Where do you want to look? We could start by the river where we first met her when we were frogs."

"That's what I thought," I said. "We'll just have to

hope she's there, because I wouldn't know where else to look."

I sat behind Eadric on Bright Country when we left a short time later. We tried to make our plans on the way, which was difficult since we really didn't know what to expect.

"So we're just going to ask the fairy to end the curse, is that right?" Eadric asked.

"That's the first thing we'll try," I said.

"What will you do if she refuses? She will, you know. She's that kind of fairy."

"I hadn't really thought that far."

"Then here's what I suggest. Think of a spell ahead of time, and when she isn't looking, do something that will make her remove the curse."

"Even if I wanted to do something like that, it wouldn't work on a fairy. Witches' magic never does."

"Have you ever tried it?" Eadric asked.

"No, but—"

"Then how do you know it wouldn't work?"

"Because Grassina taught me a long time ago that fairies aren't affected by ordinary magic. Their magic is completely different from ours." I usually enjoyed Eadric's company, but sometimes he could be so annoying.

Eadric grunted and said, "Do you have another plan?"

"Yes, but it's not nearly as good as the first one."

"We are in trouble, then, aren't we?"

"I sincerely hope not," I said, but I had a feeling that he was right.

The last time we'd gone to the river, Eadric and I had been frogs and Aunt Grassina had carried us. The trip was much faster this time, partly because we were on horseback, partly because we knew where we were going. It wasn't long before we saw the river through the trees ahead, although it took a bit of hunting to find the place where we'd met the fairy. When we found a clearing that looked promising, Eadric jumped down, then helped me off Bright Country's back.

Cupping my hands around my mouth, I called, "Swamp Fairy! We need to talk to you."

"Don't you have a better name for her than Swamp Fairy?" Eadric asked. "Like Petunia or some typical fairy name?"

I shook my head. "I don't know any other name for her. Tell me if you learn of one."

"Huh," said Eadric. "It just sounds stupid, calling *Swamp Fairy* like that."

"Sorry," I said, getting even more exasperated with his unhelpful advice. Turning my back to him, I tried calling again. "Swamp Fairy, are you there?"

When there was no answer, I gritted my teeth and said, "Maybe we're in the wrong spot. Let's try down by the river."

We left the clearing, forcing our way through patches of wildflowers and scrubby-looking bushes. Thorns caught at my skirts, slowing me down, while Eadric forged on past me and reached the river first, even though he was leading Bright Country. I was about to start calling to the Swamp Fairy again when I noticed something that hadn't been there before. Someone had built a small hut beside the water only a short distance downriver. It was a cozy-looking hut, fairly new with a freshly thatched roof and a door woven out of still-green reeds.

"You don't think the Swamp Fairy lives there, do you?" Eadric asked.

I shrugged. "I suppose it's possible."

We were approaching the hut, looking for some hint of who might live in it, when Bright Country nickered, and the door to the hut flew open. A man stepped out, shading his eyes against the afternoon sun. It was Haywood.

"Hello!" he called. "Is that you, Emma, Eadric?"

"Haywood," I replied. "What are you doing here?"

"I live here now," he said, gesturing to the hut. "How do you like it? This is the house I told you about. I built it myself."

"Very nice," I said.

"Isn't this where you lived when you were an otter?" asked Eadric.

"The exact spot. I was living in town until my land-lord kicked me out. My magic kept blowing holes in his thatched roof. I had a lot of fond memories of this place, and I didn't know where else to go."

"You could have come back to my parents' castle."

"Not the way Grassina acts around me. Besides I didn't want to impose any more than I had already. Would you like to come in? It's roomy inside."

I followed him through the door while Eadric tied Bright Country's reins to a tree. "It's very nice of you to—oh my!"

It was obvious that Haywood's magic had improved. The hut that had seemed so small from the outside was spacious within and reminded me of Grassina's former room in the tower. While I knew the walls were some kind of plaster, the roof was thatched and the floor was pounded dirt, it didn't look like that to me—they all seemed to be made of stone. A large workbench stood against one wall, while a bed with a wooden frame rested in the corner. A fire burned in the fireplace, although I'd seen no sign of either a chimney or smoke from the out-side. A dog lay in front of the hearth, and it wagged its tail when it saw me.

"Olefat's visiting," said Haywood. "He can stand your grandmother for only a few days at a time. I told him he could stay here when he needs to get away."

I nodded, having recognized the animal. Olefat, the

former wizard, looked healthy and well fed.

Haywood offered us seats on his only bench. When we were settled, he sat down beside us and asked, "What brings you out this way?"

"I found out who pronounced the curse on my family," I said. "I came to ask her to remove it. You haven't seen the Swamp Fairy, have you?"

Haywood jumped to his feet. "She's the one who did it?"

Eadric nodded. "The curse said that a true love's kiss would also break the spell."

Haywood looked doubtful. "A kiss? You mean someone would have to kiss—"

"Grassina," said Eadric. "And if you still love her, that someone would have to be you. You do still love her, don't you Haywood?"

"Well," Haywood said reluctantly, "I love the sweet person she used to be, but she isn't that person anymore, is she? You know that Grassina doesn't like me. Even if I wanted to kiss her, I don't think she'd let me get close enough, although I suppose I could try it while she's sleeping."

"The curse mentioned seeing her true self in her gaze," said Eadric. "Doesn't that mean that her eyes have to be open?"

"Probably," I said. "I think the cure is about love, not whether or not you can sneak up on someone. That's why we need to see the Swamp Fairy. You haven't seen her recently, have you?"

"She takes a nap under the old willow in the afternoons. But if she's the one who cursed your ancestor, I don't think it would do you any good to talk to her. I don't know her very well, but from what I've heard about her, she's more likely to put another curse on you than she is to be of help. You might consider turning around and going home. As bad as the curse may be, there are some things that are much worse."

"I can't give up, Haywood. Grassina's always playing tricks on people and making our lives miserable. I don't think we can stand her much longer, but she has no intention of leaving. The only way I can make the castle livable again is if I change Grassina back to the way she used to be."

Haywood shook his head. "All I can say is, 'Good luck,' because you're going to need it. The old willow isn't far from here. I can show you the way, if you'd like."

Accompanied by Olefat, who had to stop and sniff all the interesting scents, Haywood led Eadric and me to a steep slope, then stopped and pointed. The slope ran down to the river, and at its base grew a willow so old that its roots seemed to be the only things holding the edge of the crumbling bank in place. Haywood left after trying to dissuade us one more time. Olefat had already scampered off, following some animal's trail.

Eadric and I climbed down the slope to the willow, but we didn't see any sign of the fairy. Wary of the insects that make willows their homes, I pushed aside the long, trailing leaves and looked again. At first glance there didn't seem to be anyone in the green-tinted world beneath the tree.

"Is that her?" asked Eadric. He gestured to a glowing dot attached to one of the gently swaying leaves.

"Swamp Fairy," I called, trying to keep my voice soft so I wouldn't startle her. "Swamp Fairy, we need to talk to you."

The dot shivered, and suddenly the full-sized Swamp Fairy was standing in front of us, rubbing her eyes and yawning. Her blue hair was disheveled and streaked with more gray than I remembered, and her flower-petal skirt was rumpled and creased. She patted her mouth when she yawned again, then said, "What do you want? Hasn't anyone ever told you to let sleeping fairies lie?"

"I thought that was sleeping dogs," said Eadric.

"Doesn't matter." After studying our faces through narrowed eyes, she said, "Say, don't I know you from somewhere?"

This was encouraging. At least she remembered us. "We met at a party a long time ago," I said.

"It must have been a long time. I don't go to parties anymore."

"It was a birthday party," said Eadric. "They served

great food."

"Really?" said the fairy, her eyes brightening.

"And excellent ale," I said.

"Oh, that party," said the Swamp Fairy. "Yes, that was a while ago. How did you get there?"

"I'm a witch," I said. "And a relative of Hazel's. That's why we're here. You laid a curse on my family when you were leaving."

The Swamp Fairy's eyes narrowed. "I remember," she said. "Your relative was very rude."

"I know, and I'm sorry. I didn't like her much, either. But it's been a long time, and we were wondering if you could remove the curse now."

The fairy shook her head. "I never remove a curse I've cast. It's admitting that you were wrong, and I'm never wrong."

"But it's been hundreds of years! Generations of my family have suffered because of your curse. Isn't that enough?"

"No, I told you. She was very rude."

"What if we gave you something in exchange?" asked Eadric. "Emma has some dragon's breath."

"Eadric, I don't think—"

"No thanks. I already have a vial full. Got it from some dumb-looking frogs awhile back."

"Dumb-looking?" Eadric said. When I saw the muscles of his jaw tightening, I knew we were in trouble.

"If you want to know what dumb-looking is, try looking in a mirror."

"Uh, Eadric…," I began.

"How dare you?" exclaimed the fairy. The air around her began to shimmer, but before she could raise her arms, Olefat the dog tore down the slope, barking at a rabbit he was chasing. Darting this away and that, the rabbit veered away from the fairy, only to have Olefat drive him back. The fairy shrieked when the rabbit ran across her feet, leaving dirty paw prints on her toes.

Grabbing hold of Eadric's belt, I hustled him away from the willow. "What are you doing?" he said after we'd scrambled up the steep embankment. "She didn't do anything about the curse yet."

"And she won't, either, not after you insulted her," I said, pulling his arm to keep him moving. "In case you didn't notice, she was about to turn you into a slug or something equally repulsive. We have to get away from here. I don't know how far a fairy can cast a curse."

Eadric and I hurried back the way we'd come, heading toward Haywood's hut. When the willow was a good distance behind us, Eadric turned to me and said, "You should have used your magic and made her remove the curse while you had the chance."

"I told you, my magic doesn't work on fairies," I snapped. "If I'd tried it, we'd *both* be slugs. We're going to have to go see Haywood again."

"What's the point?" grumbled Eadric. "He already refused to help us."

We had nearly reached Haywood's hut when Olefat trotted up beside me, a satisfied look on his doggy face. "And that," he said, "was number two!" Wagging his tail, Olefat disappeared into the underbrush.

We stopped to watch a patch of wildflowers rustle with the dog's passage. "What did he mean by that?" Eadric asked.

"I don't think he intends to be a dog for much longer. I think he's trying to do favors for strangers so he can break the spell and become human again."

"And distracting the fairy was the second one? What do you suppose the first one might have been?"

"He saved me from a cat," I said. "He was a lousy human, but he makes a very nice dog."

Haywood wasn't surprised when we told him that the fairy had refused to remove the curse. He nodded and said, "I hate to say I told you so."

"We were hoping you could help us," I said.

Haywood frowned. "I can't. Even getting Grassina to talk to me would be nearly impossible."

"You could try, couldn't you?" I asked. "If you kiss her, she'll turn back into the sweet Grassina she used to be, and you already said that she was the one you love."

"Think about it, Emma," said Haywood. "Grassina

doesn't want to have a thing to do with me and threatens me if I go anywhere near her. Who knows what she'll do if I try to force a kiss on her? She could do something to make all of us miserable, and I'd never forgive myself if something happened to you two. You'll just have to learn to live with her the way she is or find some way to get her to move."

"Please?" I asked. "It isn't just about Grassina. There's Eadric and me, too."

"Huh?" said Eadric. "What are you talking about?"

"I want to marry you, Eadric, but if we don't end the curse one way or another, I can't marry you or anyone else."

"Emma, you can't mean that! You know how much I want to marry you. I love you!"

"And I love you, too, which is why I can't marry you with the curse hanging over us. I don't want the same thing to happen to you that happened to my grandfather. I don't want you to end up married to someone so nasty that living in the dungeon is preferable to living with her."

"Just because that happened to them doesn't mean it will happen to us. We won't have any flowers near the castle and you can—"

"Eadric, it wouldn't work. There will always be the chance that I might come in contact with some by accident. Look at what happened to Grassina when my grandmother sent all those magical flowers to fall on her."

"Then we'll have to do whatever it takes to end the curse, won't we?" said Eadric. "What do you say, Haywood? Will you try?"

Haywood sighed. "If it means that there's a chance that I could get my Grassina back and that you two can get married, yes, I'll try. But I can't guarantee anything."

"We don't expect you to, do we, Eadric?"

"Well, it would be nice," Eadric muttered under his breath.

"I'll be there tomorrow," said Haywood. "I have a few things to do first."

It was dusk when Eadric and I returned to the castle, and I half expected to see Li'l out hunting for insects. The area around the castle was curiously quiet, however, and I learned why when Bright Country suddenly reared up, nearly dumping us off his back.

"What happened?" Eadric asked Bright Country, patting his neck as the horse danced nervously to the side of the road.

"Didn't you see it?" said the horse. "A huge, scaly beast just ran in front of me. It looked right at me and stuck out its tongue!"

"That was probably Grassina," I said. "She must have gone out for the evening."

"Grassina is a scaly beast now?" asked Bright Country.

I nodded. "She likes turning into a lizard. A few weeks ago, she tried being a wolf. Who knows what she'll try next."

As we'd missed supper, Eadric and I went straight to the kitchen to find something to eat. He had befriended everyone on the kitchen staff during his frequent visits there, so they were delighted to see him. After they spent a few minutes reminiscing about his last stay, the cook said, "We know where you got your appetite. Your father can eat even more than you can!"

"My parents are here?" Eadric asked.

"They arrived right before supper. 'Good timing,' I said, when I heard how hungry His Majesty was. I had to cook extra eels just for him."

Eadric grinned. "My father likes eels, but they give him awful indigestion."

"You do take after him, don't you?" I said, kissing him on the cheek. "Come on, you can introduce me."

Eadric gazed at the platters of leftovers with great longing. "All right," he said, "as long as Cook saves us some supper."

Cook laughed. "Don't worry, we'll save plenty of food. It will even be enough for you!"

We were leaving the kitchen when Eadric said to me, "I'd better warn you. My parents aren't anything like yours."

"You mean your mother is sweet and friendly?"

"I wouldn't go that far," he said, grinning again.

"Eadric, my boy!" called a deep voice, and I looked up to see a short, heavyset man with a well-rounded belly coming toward us. A tall, thin woman with frizzy, brown hair turning to gray followed at his heels.

Eadric greeted the couple, then said, "Father, Mother, this is Princess Emeralda, the girl I'm going to marry."

"This is your Emma?" said Eadric's father. "Why, she's lovely, my boy. You've found yourself a good one."

"Emma," said Eadric, "this is my father, King Bodamin, and my mother, Queen Frazzela."

"Delighted to meet you, my dear," said the queen, in a high, thin voice.

Even through the formalities of royal greetings, I noticed that the queen's nails were nibbled short, and she had permanent worry creases on her forehead. *Eadric was right,* I thought. *They aren't anything like my parents.*

Later, when Eadric and I finally had a minute alone, I said, "Your father is the first person to tell me that I'm lovely who seemed to mean it. The only people who've told me that before were ones who think they're supposed to flatter a princess."

"I think you're lovely," murmured Eadric.

"Only because you love me," I said.

"Hmm," he said, kissing me before I could say anything else.

Fourteen

The next day was overcast, with a heavy blanket of clouds blocking the sun. The tournament to celebrate my birthday was to be held in the field where Father and his knights usually practiced with their swords and lances. Carpenters had taken over the field weeks before, building stands for the crowd that would come to watch and setting up tents for the competing knights. The wooden barrier that ran the length of the tilting field and divided the field in two was also ready, its frame draped with colorful fabric.

Since I hadn't seen Eadric in the castle, I assumed he was getting ready for his first run against someone called the Black Knight. It had become fashionable for a knight to choose a color for his armor, then claim that color for his name during the tournament. Eadric's color was silver, which looked wonderful when he was on his white horse. Although I had met most of the competing knights, I didn't know which colors they had chosen.

With their helmets closed and their faces covered, I had no way of telling until after they'd competed and removed their helmets.

I was on my way to the field, hoping to see Eadric before the games began, when I saw my grandmother chatting with Oculura and her sister, Dyspepsia. Olefat the dog was also there, sniffing the hems of their gowns. As I approached the tents closest to the castle, I spotted Grassina scurrying toward the moat. She was carrying something in her arms, but I couldn't tell what it was from a distance.

The herald's trumpet blared just as I started toward my aunt. "King Limelyn has declared that all lances must be blunted for this tournament," announced the herald. "Any knight using a pointed lance will be disqualified."

My father always ordered the blunting of lances, though even blunted lances could deliver powerful blows. I'd been so preoccupied with the curse that I hadn't thought about Eadric's safety, and suddenly I was worried. The competition was dangerous, and so was the threat of the unknown magic that my grandmother and Oculura had mentioned. I decided to do something about it—nothing that would help Eadric win, because I knew he wouldn't stand for that, just something that would keep him from getting hurt.

I found a quiet spot behind two of the tents where no one could see what I was doing and reached into my purse. There wasn't much inside that was suitable, but I found a small coin that would do. Holding the coin in one hand, I recited a health-and-safety charm.

> Keep the wearer of this charm
> Safe from any kind of harm.
> Keep the wearer healthy, too.
> Bring him back as good as new.

The coin glowed bright orange for a second, then faded to its original copper. When it was dull again, I took a scarf I'd intended to give to Eadric as a token of my favor and tied the coin in one of the corners. I'd give it to him as soon as I saw him.

The festive atmosphere surrounding tournaments always attracted people from all over. Some came to compete, some to watch and others to make money. Wandering minstrels, jugglers and merchants selling food and trinkets all vied for the attention of anyone passing by. This tournament seemed to be especially popular, with commoners and nobles traveling all the way from Eadric's kingdom of Upper Montevista.

I wandered through the growing crowd looking for Eadric. Instead I ran into Haywood, who was listening to a minstrel's song about an enchanted prince.

"It's not like that at all," Haywood said when he saw me. "But you would know what I mean, having been a frog. Everyone thinks that when you're turned into an animal, you pine away for your human life. You don't, though. You get used to being an animal pretty quickly. It takes a lot longer to remember how to be a human when you turn back. I still don't have it mastered, and it's been more than a year."

"You were an otter for so long," I said.

"That's true. I'm sure it'll just take time. Let's go see Grassina and finish this. I don't like being around crowds anymore."

We found Grassina by the moat near where I'd seen her before. She was staring down into the water, muttering to herself, with her long, straggly hair hanging down around her face. Her cloak lay on the ground beside her, covering something large and lumpy.

"Aunt Grassina," I said. "There's someone here to see you."

She turned her head abruptly and peered up at Haywood through her curtain of hair. "What does he want?" she growled.

"He just wants to talk to you."

"Well, I don't want to talk to him."

Haywood cleared his throat and said, "Hello, Grassina. How have you been?"

"Good, since you left. Why don't you leave again so I can be even better?"

"There's no need to be like that, Grassina," he said.

"We haven't really talked in a long time and—"

"Not nearly long enough. Can't you see I'm busy with matters more important than talking to a brainless nit like you?"

"What are you doing, Aunt Grassina?" I asked.

"Nothing," she snarled. "Now, go away and let me do it some more."

"What is that?" If anyone was going to ill-use magic at the tournament, it was bound to be Grassina. I reached for her cloak, but she slapped my hand aside.

"Keep your hands to yourself if you don't want to lose them," she said, spitting out the words.

"Aunt Grassina," I tried one more time. "I found out how to end the curse."

"What curse? You mean being cursed with rotten relatives who won't leave you alone? Or cursed with nincompoops who have smaller brains than fleas do and don't know when to quit? What do I have to do to get rid of you two? I'd turn into a lizard and eat you both if I wasn't so busy. Now, leave me alone before I turn you into worms and toss you into the moat. I'm not too busy for that!"

"But Aunt Grassina!"

"Now!" she barked, pointing a finger at us as she began to mutter a spell.

I could have counteracted any spell she tried on me, but that wouldn't make her any nicer. Remembering the wording of the curse, I was sure a forced kiss wouldn't do any good. The way Grassina was acting, there wouldn't be any other kind. "Let's go, Haywood," I said, hustling him away from my aunt. "We'll come back when she's in a better mood."

"I'm in a wonderful mood now, you ninny!" my aunt shouted as we hurried toward the tilting field, "because you two are leaving!"

We didn't stop until we reached the first of the tents, and Haywood turned to me to say, "It's no use, Emma. I wouldn't be able to get close enough to that woman to kiss her even if I wanted to. The only reason I was willing to try was to help you and Eadric, and that probably wasn't enough to break the curse, anyway. I'm sorry, Emma. I'm going home."

I was feeling desperate. After everything I had gone through, the curse was as strong as ever. "Are you sure, Haywood? You know she acts like that because of the curse. That wasn't the real Grassina back there. Maybe it would be different next time."

Haywood shook his head. "She seemed real enough to me. You know she's not going to change. Good-bye, Emma. You and Eadric should come visit me sometime."

I headed toward the stands, feeling more dejected than I'd ever felt before. I dreaded having to tell Eadric that I couldn't marry him after all. Even worse, I was going to have to live with an aunt who was getting nastier by the day. If only Grassina could have been nice for just a few minutes!

I glanced back and saw my aunt bending down, pouring something from a big jug into the water. *She's up to something,* I thought, and turned around. By the time I reached the moat, however, Grassina had already gathered her cloak and jug and scuttled off toward the drawbridge.

Kneeling beside the water, I tried to peer into its depths, but all I saw were green bubbles rising to the surface. I was considering using a spell to call up whatever Grassina had put in there when I heard the strident notes of the heralds' trumpets above the clamor of the crowd. I sighed and brushed off my skirts, knowing that I'd have to figure out what Grassina had done later. The tournament was about to start, and Eadric was in the first round.

I found my seat in the stands between my mother and Queen Frazzela. Mother nodded approvingly at the yellow gown I wore, one of the new ones she'd had the seamstress make while I was in the past. Queen Frazzela gave me a halfhearted smile, but she seemed too worried to be enjoying herself.

"I hate tournaments," she said. "Someone always gets hurt. At least Bodi no longer competes." She patted her husband's hand where it rested on the arm of his chair beside her. I wondered how the portly, little man had ever fit into a suit of armor. He smiled at his wife reassuringly, then turned back to the approaching knights. Dressed in silver armor, Eadric rode Bright Country, who pranced alongside the Black Knight's all-black charger as if he was having a wonderful time.

"If only Eadric would stop competing," said his mother.

"There, there, my dear," said King Bodamin. "It's good for the boy. And before you know it, Bradston here will be ready." The king patted the head of a boy about ten years old seated at his other side. "Princess Emeralda," said the king, "this is our younger son, Bradston." The boy smiled at his father, but the king had already looked away so he didn't notice that the smile dissolved into a scowl as Bradston smoothed his hair back into place. Sticking his tongue out at me, he rolled his eyes up in his head and shoved back the tip of his nose with one finger so he looked like a pig.

I'd heard about Eadric's younger brother. It was because of Bradston that Eadric had met the witch who'd turned him into a frog.

"It's nice to meet you, Prince Bradston," I said. For the first time in my life, I was glad that I was an only child.

"You'll have to excuse Brad the Brat," said a voice, and I looked up to see Eadric smiling at me from Bright

Country's back. "He usually falls asleep during the lessons on courtly manners."

I smiled and reached into my purse for the scarf. "This is for you," I said, handing it to Eadric.

He grinned and tucked it under the neck of his armor. "Thank you, my lady. I shall wear your token by my heart." Bradston made a rude noise, which we all pretended not to hear.

Wondering who Eadric was competing against, I glanced at the Black Knight, but his visor covered his face. After saluting both royal couples, the knights turned their horses and trotted down the field, taking up their positions at opposite ends of the tilting barrier.

I sat up straighter when trumpets blared and the herald announced, "The Silver Knight shall ride against the Black Knight!" then held my breath when they lowered their lances and charged.

I'd never seen Eadric joust before, although I had seen him fight a monstrous spider with his sword. He had told me that he was good with a lance as well, but I didn't know how good until he charged down that field. His back straight, his lance poised, his horse's hooves pounding the turf, Eadric looked like the kind of knight in shining armor that every princess dreams about. He was perfect for me, so perfect that he made my heart ache. I'd still have to tell him that I couldn't marry him.

I gasped when the knights' lances slammed into their

opponents' armor. Both lances splintered and the knights rode on, unharmed. They rode again with fresh lances in their hands. Once again, the lances splintered, the sound of the impacts making me wince. On the third round, the Black Knight's lance splintered and broke while Eadric's held firm, knocking his opponent off his saddle. The Black Knight landed on his back with a thud that shook the ground and made my heart skip a beat. Although I was rooting for Eadric, I bit my lip until the Black Knight stirred and some eager squires helped him to his feet. I hated seeing anyone get hurt.

I glanced at Queen Frazzela. Her face was pale, and beads of perspiration had formed on her upper lip. "Eadric will be fine," I said, thinking of my health-and-safety charm.

"If only I knew that for certain!" said his mother.

Although I was tempted to tell her about the charm, I didn't dare because I didn't know how much Eadric had told her about me. Given a choice, I'd rather not be the one to inform her that I was a witch.

While Eadric trotted off to wait for his next turn, the Red Knight rode up to take his place. To everyone's surprise, another knight in silver armor forced his way past the milling squires, taking up the opposite position. When the herald approached, the noise of the crowd died away.

"You may announce me as the Silver Knight," said

the new arrival.

"You can't be the Silver Knight," said the herald. "We already have one. There's only one of a color allowed per tournament, so you'll have to go."

"And if I come back in another color?" asked the knight, his voice muffled by his lowered visor.

"That would be fine," said the herald.

Turning his gray charger back the way he'd come, the knight rode off the field just as the Blue Knight arrived. A large man, he looked imposing in his deep blue armor astride his chestnut steed. However, after the second round he, too, lay flat on his back staring up at the sky.

The Blue Knight had scarcely been helped from the field when the knight on the gray charger was back. Armored in black, he rode into position and waited for the herald to announce him. Once again the crowd fell silent as the herald approached the knight.

"You can't wear that color, either," said the herald. "We've already had a Black Knight. You're going to have to find a color no one else has claimed."

"But I don't have any other armor with me," protested the knight.

The herald shrugged. "The court armorer might have something you can borrow."

The knight leaned forward and tried to speak in a confidential tone, although I could still hear him. "Are you sure I can't wear this?" he asked the herald. "I hate wearing borrowed armor. You never know who's worn it or if it's been properly cleaned."

"Sorry, Sir Knight," said the herald. "Rules are rules. I'm sure one of the young lads would be happy to show you the way."

"If I must," grumbled the knight, yanking the reins so his horse reared up and the herald was forced to jump aside.

When it was time for Eadric to ride again, Bright Country pranced to his place at the end of the tilting barrier, obviously enjoying himself. I was expecting the Gold Knight when the knight on the gray horse returned. His armor was an unusual color, a mix of brown and purple. This time an expectant murmur ran through the crowd as the herald approached him.

"Now, that's a different color," said the herald, smiling broadly. "How do you want me to announce you?"

"As the Purple Knight, of course," said the knight.

"But that's not purple," offered a squire standing nearby.

"This is ridiculous!" said the knight. "I don't care what you call it! Just announce me."

The herald grinned. "Whatever you say, Sir Knight." The herald sounded his trumpet once more, then shouted, "Lords and ladies, gentlemen and gentle-women. The Puce Knight!"

Shouts of laughter rocked the stands. Pennants

waved in the air as the squires holding them chortled and guffawed. Apparently this angered the Puce Knight. He spurred his horse until the silk covering its flanks tore and blood trickled. Rounding the end of the tilt barrier, he took up his position and waited, his lance aimed and ready.

Once again I held my breath as Eadric rode into position. When the trumpet sounded, the two horses charged, their hooves thundering in unison. The lances hit with resounding thwacks and both knights flew off their horses, landing on their backs in the dust.

I jumped to my feet, but I couldn't see through the press of bodies that had quickly surrounded Eadric. Some men helped the Puce Knight stand, and I began to worry when Eadric didn't stand as well.

"Sit down, Emeralda," said my mother. "The men will see to him."

"But why isn't he standing yet?" I said. "He should be up by now."

With a sigh and a soft thump, Eadric's mother fainted. Everyone rushed to help her, so no one noticed when I slipped under the railing and ran to Eadric. I was nearly there when the Puce Knight reached him.

Eadric lay on his back, the Puce Knight's lance protruding from his armor. Someone had already removed Eadric's helmet and I could see the pallor of his face beneath his sweat-matted hair. The crowd was muttering about pointed lances when the Puce Knight grabbed hold of the lance and pulled it free.

Eadric groaned and lifted his head. "What happened?" he asked.

The Puce Knight raised his lance and slammed it into Eadric's armor. We heard a strange twanging sound, and the lance bounced back. Eadric looked bewildered, but he didn't seem the least bit hurt.

Two of the men standing nearby restrained the Puce Knight while others helped Eadric to his feet. "Let me see that!" Eadric said, grabbing the lance from the Puce Knight's hands. "Emma!" he called, looking for me in the crowd. When people turned and saw me, they moved aside and let me through. "What do you make of this?" he asked, showing me the lance.

It was sharpened, just as I'd thought, but that wasn't all. Holding my hand over the lance, I could feel the magic surrounding it. "Someone has strengthened the point with a spell."

"The point, huh?" said Eadric. "Then let's see what this does." Taking the lance in both hands, he slammed the shaft against his armor-clad knee, breaking it neatly in two. "Now let's see who's hiding behind this helmet."

The Puce Knight struggled to get away, but two burly men held him tightly as Eadric lifted the helmet from the knight's head. I gasped when I saw his face. It was Prince Jorge, the son of the king who had led the invasion of

Greater Greensward the previous summer and the man my mother had wanted me to marry before I met Eadric.

"Jorge!" I said. "Why did you do this?"

Jorge looked from Eadric to me, his eyes hard and angry. "You two humiliated the royal house of East Aridia. It was time you learned a lesson."

"So you tried to kill Eadric?" I said. "What kind of lesson was that?"

"A good one," said Jorge, looking smug. "I thought of it myself."

I hadn't noticed that the crowd had parted for my father until I heard him say, "Arrest that man!" The captain of the guard led the way as three of his men hustled Prince Jorge off the field.

While the men-at-arms herded the crowd back to the stands, Eadric turned to me. "What just happened? Why didn't that lance kill me?"

"Remember that token I gave you?" I asked. "I put a health-and-safety charm on it. The air was knocked out of you when you fell, but Jorge couldn't do any real damage to you as long as you carried that scarf."

Eadric frowned. "I thought it might be something like that. Here, take it back," he said, reaching into his armor. "It isn't a fair fight if I have an advantage."

"But Eadric, Jorge wasn't trying to fight fairly. He wanted to kill you!"

"And now he's under arrest and we don't have to

worry about him, do we? Promise me you won't ever do anything like that again. I don't want you to use magic for me unless you ask me first. Do you promise?"

"If I have to," I said. "But I don't think it's right. I was only trying to keep you safe."

"I know," he said, kissing me on the tip of my nose. "And that's why I'm not really mad. Just don't do it again. Understand?"

"Yes," I grumbled.

Eadric's fall had shaken his mother so badly that she insisted he quit the field for the day, nagging him until he agreed. Then, complaining of a headache, she went back to the castle to rest, taking Bradston with her. Since he was no longer participating in the jousting contest, Eadric removed his armor and took his mother's place in the seat beside me.

The jousting contest was far from over, although the rest felt like an anticlimax to me. Before any more knights met on the tilting field, my father had them all come before him with their helmets off. "Just so we know who's here," he said.

The only surprise was the Black Knight. When he took off his helmet, he was a stranger to everyone except Eadric and me. It was Prince Garrid, the vampire we'd met in Hazel's time.

I gasped and sat forward in my seat. "Garrid, what are you doing here?" I asked.

He smiled. "Hello, Emma. You don't know how relieved I am that I finally found you. I've been waiting for you for years."

"For me?" I asked, confused.

"Actually, I've been waiting for Li'l, but I knew I'd find her only if I could find you. She told me about a lot of things, including this tournament. That's how I knew when to look for you."

"But why?" I knew that vampires were immortal, yet trying to find a particular bat after all those years didn't seem to make much sense.

"Because I realized that Li'l was my one true love. I never married Hazel or anyone else. No one could compare with my Li'l."

"Li'l? Who's that?" asked my mother.

"A friend of mine," I replied. "I met her shortly after I met Eadric."

Mother frowned, her expression changing to one of astonishment when she realized what kind of friend Li'l might be. I'd made a number of friends when I was a frog, and they'd all been animals. "Does she live around here?" she asked, looking at me suspiciously.

"Up in my tower," I said. "Garrid, if you'd like to go see her, she's taking a nap in the storage room right now."

"In the storage room?" Mother echoed, her face turning pale.

I pointed at the castle. "It's the tall tower on the

right," I told the prince.

Grinning, Garrid saluted me and left, his armor clanking all the way across the field.

My mother tugged on my sleeve. "How will he get into the tower chamber? You always keep that door locked."

"He'll find a way," I said, glancing at the tower windows. It wouldn't be any problem for a bat.

Fifteen

J'd begun to relax, certain that Jorge's lance had been the magical threat Oculura and my grandmother had warned me about, when Eadric leaned toward me and said, "I saw Grassina when I was coming out of my tent. Why is your aunt strewing pieces of raw chicken on the ground? She was making a lot of dogs happy until she chased them away with her broom."

I jumped to my feet and looked toward Eadric's tent. "Where was she headed?"

"I don't know," he said. "I—"

A woman shrieked. At first I thought it might be a peacock, but when the ground shook and other people started screaming, I knew I'd let my guard down too soon.

While I tried to see what was going on, Eadric hurdled the railing. "You stay here," he said.

I slipped under the railing and started running. "I'm the Green Witch, remember?" I shouted over my shoulder. "I don't stay out of trouble; I take care of it."

Eadric yanked Ferdy from his scabbard and ran to catch up with me. "How could I forget?" he yelled.

I was still in front of the viewing stand when the tent at the end shivered. Looking up, I saw an enormous gray tentacle rise above the green roof, then smack down its peak, squashing the tent flat. A few people—unlucky enough to have been caught inside—squirmed out from under the fabric walls. I hoped that there was no one left behind.

Eadric had always been the faster runner, so he reached the pavilion first. This time when the tentacle swept down out of the sky, he was ready for it and grabbed hold with one arm, twisting his body so he could wrap his legs around it. Hanging on with all his strength, Eadric rode it up into the sky, where it thrashed back and forth, trying to shake him off.

I couldn't make up a spell to fight it until I knew exactly what I was fighting, so I ran around the flattened pavilion, hoping to get a better look at the creature. There was a whoosh of air above me and I heard Eadric shout. Looking up, I saw him riding the tentacle as if it was a wild, bucking horse. I was so close that I could hear Ferdy singing as Eadric hacked at his ghastly, gray steed.

Slash, hack, chop and whack.
Cut down the foe, he'll not come back.

Slash, hack, chop and whack.

No monster shall hurt my master.

Pieces of its flesh dropped from the sky, but the tentacle kept flailing, smashing tents and flinging tent poles and cart wheels through the air. People screamed and scattered as the creature moved toward the tilting field.

"Emma," called Eadric from somewhere above my head, "let me have that token."

"Are you sure?" I hollered. "You made me promise."

"Forget the promise," he yelled. "Just send it to me!"

"Fine," I said to myself. "And they say women can't make up their minds."

Taking the coin and scarf in one hand, I sent it to Eadric with a flick of my fingers and a few whispered words. The scarf shivered, then spread out like the wings of a bird and began to flap, carrying the coin up to Eadric. It took a while for it to reach him because the tentacle kept moving, but he finally saw the scarf coming and grabbed it as he whipped past.

Hearing a loud hiss, I dashed around one of the few tents that was still standing, past a fleeing troop of jugglers headed the other way and found what I was looking for. The enormous creature carrying Eadric lurched across the ground, dragged by tentacles that had never been intended for dry land. Half again as wide as the biggest tent, the monster had the hard-shelled body of a crab, the sharp-faced head of a shark and the tentacles of an enormous octopus. It was a composite of three different creatures. Now I knew what I had to do; I just had to find a way to do it.

Two knights were trying to drive the monster back with their lances, but the shell-covered body was too hard to penetrate and the shark's head too fierce to approach. When it snapped at them, its shark's teeth clanged against their already dented armor. Shattered lances littered the ground, and the hafts of their broken swords jutted uselessly from the monster's mouth.

Eadric must have seen this as he tore through the sky, for the next time the tentacle carried him over the monster's body he let go and leapt onto its back. The shark's jaws gaped as the body shook, trying to dislodge Eadric.

A horse screamed, and I turned to see another knight spur his destrier straight at the lurching monster. When the shark's head turned and lunged, the poor warhorse reared up, nearly dumping the knight onto the ground. The horse whirled, and the last thing we saw of the knight was the back of his armor, bouncing wildly as his steed galloped between the remaining tents and out of sight.

Unlike the monsters Grassina had created before, this was a composite monster created out of three innocent creatures. Leaving them in this form would not only make them miserable for the rest of their lives, but would introduce a new, more horrible beast into the world of monsters. I needed a spell that would separate the monster into its individual forms.

While Eadric tried to drag himself onto the back of the monster's head, I pointed at it and said,

> Take this monster. Make it three
> Separate creatures. You will see
> They'll be happy once again
> When they live in their own skins.

The monster lurched again and the spell missed its mark. I was trying to think of a way to get the spell where I wanted it to go when Eadric threw himself forward and landed on the shark's head. The monster snapped at him, but Eadric ducked, jamming Ferdy into the spot where the shark's head joined the shell. He was trying to drive Ferdy in farther when one of the monster's tentacles wrapped itself around his waist, plucked him off and tossed him aside like a broken doll. I cried out as he flew through the air, his arms and legs flailing.

Eadric was yelling when he hit the ground, but instead of a solid thump, he hit with a squishy kind of sound and immediately bounced back onto his feet.

"Wow!" he said, when I ran to make sure he was all right. "That was incredible!"

"Eadric, I know what we need to do—" I began.

"Yeah, but did you see that? I was flying, and then I hit the ground, and I bounced and then—"

"Eadric, are you listening to me? That's a composite monster. I can render it harmless if I can break it up into its individual parts again, but I need you to help me deliver the spell."

"I can handle that," said Eadric.

"I'll put the spell in a ball like the ones we used when we fought King Beltran and turned his soldiers into frogs and mice. You'll need to aim for a spot where you'll hit parts of all three creatures. Do you think you can do that?"

"With the charm you gave me, I think I can do anything."

"Then here goes," I said. Shaping a ball with my hands, I repeated the spell that would break the monster apart. The whole time I was working, I could hear two knights fighting the beast. I was almost finished when the monster flung them into the sides of a tent. The tent broke their fall as they flattened it to the ground. They were wallowing in the fabric when I handed Eadric the spell-filled ball.

"How sturdy is this thing?" he asked, taking it from my hands.

"Strong enough," I said. "Just don't drop it."

A high-pitched cackle grated on my nerves. Glancing

toward the tents, I spotted Grassina peeking out from behind a shattered cart, watching her creation with a mother's pride. When the monster noticed Eadric's approach, it turned its head to snap at him. Grassina chortled and rubbed her hands together. When Eadric dodged aside and tried again, she fairly danced with joy. But when he ran straight at the monster's head and tossed the ball with all the strength he could muster, she stopped laughing, her eyes clouded over and she began to mutter a spell of her own.

"Oh, no you don't!" I said and recited a binding spell.

Grassina's hand froze in mid-gesture. Her face turned nearly purple as she realized what I'd done. The only things she could move were her eyes, but she glared at me with a fierceness that said everything. The binding spell was an old one that I was sure Grassina knew, but it would take her a minute or two to break it, giving my own spell enough time to work.

The ball hit the monster, bursting with a shower of green droplets. Eadric tried to jump out of the way, but he'd underestimated the monster's reach, and the daggerlike teeth closed over his back and shoulder. Then, between one breath and the next, the monster shivered and dissolved in a lavender puddle.

Eadric stumbled and nearly fell while Ferdy clattered to the ground. Grassina howled wordlessly, the binding spell not fully broken.

The monster was gone, leaving a tiny crab, a baby octopus and a miniature shark floundering on the hard-packed dirt. They would die if we left them on the ground, so I sent them home with a quick spell. They disappeared in a green haze smelling strongly of salt water.

"How dare you?" screamed Grassina, finally getting her voice back. "That was the best monster I'd ever made! You ruined it! Now I'm going to have to start again and—"

"No, you're not," I said, glaring back at her. "Your monster-making days are over."

Grassina sneered at me. "Oh, really? And I suppose you're the one who's going to stop me?"

"If she doesn't, I will," said my grandmother, who suddenly appeared beside me. "Why did you have to ruin this tournament, you good-for-nothing, spoiled brat? You know how much I love tournaments! I used to watch your father joust before you were even a twinkle in his eye. You did this just to spite me."

"Maybe I don't like tournaments and all the noise and partying. Did you ever think of that? Or maybe I wanted to see your expression when my monster ate those precious knights."

"Or maybe you're just so cantankerous you can't stand to see anyone enjoying herself," I muttered under my breath.

"Mind your own business," Grassina said, scowling at me. Once again I'd forgotten how good Grassina's hearing could be. "Did you invite the old hag so she could help you spoil my fun? It won't do either of you any good. The feeble, old bag of bones hasn't helped anyone in years. Her magic is so pitiful that—"

"Who are you calling a feeble bag of bones, you low-life fleck of pond scum," growled my grandmother. "I'll teach you to mess with me. My magic is stronger than yours any day!" Pointing at the ground beneath Grassina's feet, my grandmother muttered a few obscure words. The ground began to rumble, and a small crack opened up.

Eadric had come up beside me when I wasn't looking. "I don't think Grassina was really thinking of your grandmother when she—"

I clapped my hand over his mouth before he could say another word. "Shh, Eadric! Not now." The last thing I wanted was for two fighting witches to turn their attention to him.

Looking back at my aunt, I saw that the crack had widened, forcing her to stumble out of the way. "Is that all you can do?" she taunted, waggling her finger almost playfully. Grassina raised her arms to the sky and began to spin in place, slowly at first, then faster and faster until she was a whirling blur. A wind began to blow, bringing dancing snowflakes with it. The snow grew thicker, swirling out in a horizontal blizzard.

I turned my head to keep the snow from blinding me and saw my grandmother stomp her feet and gesture. Suddenly there was another kind of blizzard that made us back away. A swarm of insects had formed between Grandmother's hands, pouring forth in a stinging, biting, hopping, crawling, flying cloud that roiled and swirled toward my aunt.

The snowstorm grew fiercer, freezing insects in the air and on the ground, but when a few made it past her snowy barrier, Grassina slapped at them and called up another weapon, letting her snowstorm die down to a few drifting flakes. Birds of every shape and size flocked to her, dropping out of the sky from miles around to devour the insects before turning their beady eyes on my grandmother.

"So that's how you want to play," said my grandmother, and within moments an army of cats descended on us. Snarling, screeching, stalking cats—from stable cats to lions with shaggy manes—seemed to appear out of nowhere, batting at the birds as they flew and pouncing on them when they landed.

Nearly everyone had been scared off the field by Grassina's monster. When the big cats ran out of birds to chase, they began to stalk the few humans who were still around. A tawny-coated cat with irregular spots stared at me and licked its lips. I had to do something, and I had to do it fast before things got even more out of hand. I thought of turning myself into a huge dog to chase the cats away, but Grassina beat me to it by calling up a pack of enormous wolves, exactly the kind I'd chased out of the kingdom only a few weeks before. The wolves ignored Grassina, my grandmother and me, but I knew it wouldn't be long before they turned on us as well, and if we weren't there to stop them, they'd go after anyone who stepped outside the castle walls.

"Stop it!" I shouted at my aunt and my grandmother, trying to make myself heard over the fighting. Neither paid me any attention.

I had to do something to get them to stop fighting, something they couldn't ignore. There was only one creature that I knew they both respected. I'd never turned into one before, but then I'd never tried.

> Dragons big and dragons small,
> Fiercest creatures of them all,
> Change me into one of these.
> Do it quickly, if you please.

When my skin began to burn, I wondered if I'd made a horrible mistake. Maybe people were never meant to turn into dragons. When my stomach felt like it was on fire, I was convinced that my mistake was going to be fatal. Why couldn't I have chosen a nonmagical creature?

Instead of the tingling or bubbly feeling that I usually felt when I changed, turning into a dragon was painful. Everything about me hurt: my skin, my stomach, my head, my muscles, even my bones. The pain grew worse until I felt as though I'd been dipped in molten lava. I was lying on the ground, writhing in agony, when the pain ended as abruptly as it had begun. *I must be dead,* I thought, opening my eyes, but I was still on the field between the moat and the tents. The fight had stopped for the moment, and everyone was staring at me.

I looked down and saw why. I was a dragon just as I wanted to be, but I wasn't quite like any dragon I'd ever seen. From the tip of my pointed snout to the end of my ridged tail, my body was an iridescent peridot green. My finger-length claws were a dark emerald color, and my pale green wings were translucent. As I'd learned months before, there were no green dragons, yet that was exactly what I had become. I was nearly twelve feet long and covered with scales, but for the first time in my life, I felt beautiful.

While everyone stared at me, I raised my wings and flexed them to see if they really worked. I didn't move them very much, but I still created a wind strong enough to send some of the smaller cats flying and blow away the last of the insects.

"Emma, is that you?" asked my aunt.

"Yes," I said, my voice sounding like a hiss.

Grandmother scratched her head. "That's not possible," she said. "No witch has ever been able to turn herself into a dragon. It must be an illusion."

"Does this feel like an illusion to you?" I asked, spreading my wings again and beating them one, two, three times. Grandmother's gown streamed out behind her, and she had to brace her feet to keep from being blown over.

"I guess not," she said, blinking at the dust I'd blown into her eyes.

Grassina sneezed, then blew her nose on her sleeve. "How is it possible?" she asked.

"It's magic," I told her. I didn't really know, either, but I suspected that it had something to do with my being a Dragon Friend.

Neither Grassina nor Grandmother protested when I herded them together and said, "No more fighting with magic. If you don't agree about something, you're going to have to learn to talk about it. Do you understand?" They nodded, their heads wobbling as if pulled by cords. "Now go to the castle and stay there until you can work this out."

They stumbled off together, glancing back at me now and then to make sure I was still behind them. I followed them as far as the drawbridge, then sat down and watched them trudge inside. "Go get started," I called after them. "I'll be right there."

My voice must have been loud in the enclosed space, because they flinched when I spoke, then scuttled away like pages caught stealing tarts from the kitchen. I flexed my wings once more, enjoying the supple way they stretched. Unfortunately I didn't have time to try them out, but I promised myself that I would turn back into a dragon as soon as I had the time to experiment.

When my aunt and my grandmother were out of sight, I repeated the spell to turn myself back into my human form. Eadric had stayed behind, but now that I was myself again, he joined me at the drawbridge. "That was easier than I expected," I said. "Did you see how they listened to me?"

Eadric licked his lips and tried to smile. "Anyone would have listened to you when you looked like that. You scared them so badly that they couldn't do other-wise. To be honest, you scared me, too!"

"Sorry about that. I just wanted them to stop fighting. It seems that's the only way those two can relate to each other anymore. I wish I could order Grassina to kiss Haywood, but I doubt it would help now. She wouldn't really mean it, and I think it has to be heartfelt to work. We'd better go see what Grassina and my grandmother are up to," I said, kissing Eadric on the cheek.

I could hear them arguing long before I reached the Great Hall. Their voices were shrill and carried well. When I entered the room, I saw that I wasn't the only one they'd attracted. Oculura and Dyspepsia were seated on a bench at the back of the room, sharing a trencher of roast goose and onions while listening to the argument. My parents were also there along with Queen Frazzela and King Bodamin, both of whom were dressed for travel.

"A forest of stinging nettles," said my grandmother. "That's what I would have tried next if Emma hadn't been there."

Grassina snorted. "You are so old-fashioned. Stinging nettles went out of style years ago! I would have tried quicksand or maybe a fog so dense that—"

"Not around my castle, you wouldn't," said a hollow-sounding voice as my grandfather materialized in the center of the room. "This isn't a testing ground for new spells. It's a home and a seat of government, which you two seem to forget. Grassina, I found out about that dust you've been using on the ghosts in the dungeon. I'm acting on behalf of the Council of Ghosts when I say that you may no longer use it under penalty of personal haunting. I've sent the affected ghosts to be purged of the dust. There will be no more tomfoolery like that around here again. It's time you and your mother grew up and started to help Emma instead of making things harder for her. Curse or no curse, you're still family."

Everyone turned their heads when Queen Frazzela groaned on the other side of the room. Her face was pale and she had her hand pressed to her throat, but that didn't stop her from speaking her mind. "This is a horrid family!" she said, her voice turning as shrill as my aunt's and grandmother's. "When I came inside to lie down, I heard the commotion, so I climbed up to the battlements. I saw everything that's gone on here today. Witches for relatives, monsters in the moat and ghosts in the castle! Even that girl is a witch," she said, pointing an accusing finger at me. "After meeting all of you, I will never give my son permission to marry into such a horrid family, regardless of how much he says he loves your princess."

My grandfather's color deepened to a rich blue as he floated toward Eadric's mother. "You have no idea what you're talking about," he said with more feeling in his voice than I'd heard in a long time. "This family may be unique, but it's not horrid." Raising his transparent arm, Grandfather pointed at my grandmother. "This woman was the best wife any man could ever have, king or not. She loved me with all her heart, but I was too busy to notice. We argued over something inconsequential, and I thought I'd make up for it with a silly bouquet of flowers. It was my fault that she fell prey to the awful curse that changed her life. If I'd known her better, it would never have happened. I loved that woman then, and I love her still. If there is such a thing as a soul mate, then this woman is mine. Any man could count himself fortunate if he could marry into this family, and he'd be a fool to think otherwise."

"Aldrid?" said my grandmother.

Grandfather turned to face her, floating back across the room until his aura nearly touched her. "I should have told you how I felt years ago, but other things always seemed to get in the way. However nasty you might have been, I've always known it was the curse talking and not you. I love you, Olivene. I always have, and I always will."

Grandfather moved toward her again, the blue of his aura engulfing her as his arms seemed to wrap around her body. Although we could see through him, we could also see when he kissed her full on the lips, and she responded, trying to kiss him back.

Tears pricked my eyes, and I was wiping them away when Eadric nudged me and said, "Will you look at that!"

A hole seemed to have opened in the ceiling, and through it streamed a shower of flower petals of every description. They fell around us, drifting onto our faces, our clothing and down to the floor. My mother shrieked and hid her face in my father's shoulder, but for the first time in centuries flower petals had no power to change the women of the royal family of Greater Greensward.

Someone laughed, a light tinkling sound that

brought a smile to everyone's lips. It was my grandmother, her face restored to her former beauty—older, sadder, but still the face that my grandfather had loved. I looked at my aunt and she had changed as well, her face the one that I had missed so much. Hearing the laughter, my mother looked up, and I saw her face transform. Years seemed to drop away from her as she realized the truth. The family curse was over.

Everyone started to laugh, a joyous sound that hadn't been heard in the castle for far too long. Still laughing, I turned to Eadric, the words I'd wanted to say already on my tongue.

Something thudded by the door, and I heard a voice cry out, "Stop it! Let go of me!" A moment later Olefat the dog backed into the room, his teeth clenching someone's sleeve. Instead of letting go, Olefat snarled and shook his head, then braced his feet and pulled even harder. With one last yank, Haywood popped through the door. When he saw everyone, he looked around sheepishly and said, "I didn't mean to intrude. The dog—" And then his eyes fell on Grassina. The astonishment on his face lasted but an instant, chased away by a look of such longing that I felt as if we were the ones who were intruding. "Grassina?" he asked. "Is that really you?"

"Oh, Haywood," she said, and suddenly they were holding each other. Olefat yipped and hopped up onto an empty bench. "And that," he said, "makes three!"

"What does he mean by…. Oh!" said Haywood as a tiny whirlwind danced around Olefat the dog, leaving Olefat the wizard in his place.

"Awk!" said Metoo the parrot, perched on the old man's shoulder. "It's about time!"

"Why are you complaining?" demanded Olefat. "I was the one who did all the work. You were just my flea!"

Taking Eadric's hand in mine, I led him to an empty corner of the room where we could have a little privacy. "The curse is over," I said before wrapping my arms around him.

"Mmm," he said. "Does that mean that we can get married now?"

I nodded. "Nothing would make me happier."

"Nothing?" he asked.

"Well," I said, "I would like to hold the ceremony in the swamp. We'll have to invite all our friends. You know who I mean. There's Li'l, of course, and Garrid if they're still together and some of the ghosts in the dungeon. Then there's Fang and—"

"What about my parents?" he asked.

"We'll have to invite them, too," I said. "They may not like me now, but you know they'll love me after they get to know me a little better."

"Of course they will," he said, kissing me on the forehead. "People always do."